get well soon

get well soon

julie halpern

FEIWEL AND FRIENDS
New York

A FEIWEL AND FRIENDS Book
An Imprint of Holtzbrinck Publishers

Library of Congress Cataloging-in-Publication Data

Halpern, Julie,
Get well soon / Julie Halpern.
p. cm.
Summary: When her parents confine her to a mental hospital, an overweight teenage girl, who suffers from panic attacks, describes her experiences in a series of letters to a friend.
ISBN 13: 978-0-312-36795-4 / ISBN 10: 0-312-36795-3
[1. Psychiatric hospitals—Fiction. 2. Mental illness—Fiction.
3. Self-perception—Fiction. 4. Letters—Fiction.] I. Title.
PZ7.H1666Ge 2007 [Fic]—dc22 2006032358

First Edition: October 2007
10 9 8 7 6 5 4 3 2 1

Book design by Kristina Albertson

www.feiwelandfriends.com

For Tracy,
who wrote me letters every day

And for Matt,
who's way dreamier
than any boy in a book

get well soon

Day 1

I AM SITTING AT A DESK IN THE MIDDLE OF A HALLWAY, and all of the lights are off. No one will tell me what they're going to do with me or how they're going to help me or how long I have to be here. They just plunked me down in this freaky place, told my parents not to worry, and now I'm stuck.

They told me to write. Write down your feelings. It'll help you. Have some paper. Have a pencil, they said. I don't like pencils, I told them. They smudge. I once kept a journal all in pencil, and when I went back to read all of the depressing stuff that I wrote, it was gone. Smudged away. I wrote it all down, the stories of my life, my feelings, all of the crap you're supposed to say in journals so you can look back and see what a big loser you used to be. But it was all gone, mushed together as if none of it mattered in the first place. Which it didn't. Because I still wound up here.

Screw journals. I don't need a journal to tell myself what I already know: Life sucks. I'm fat. Nothing interesting ever happens to me. I don't want to deal with that shit anymore.

So I'm not going to keep my thoughts around. I'm going to send them away. I'm going to write my thoughts in letters, like I did when my sister went to overnight camp. That way they're gone. Someone else has them, and I don't have to look back and see how pathetic I once was. I will write letters and I won't feel so bad. I won't feel so bad that I'm depressed. I won't feel so bad that I'm fat. And maybe, just maybe, I won't feel so bad that my parents had me locked up in this fucking mental hospital.

Friday, Day 1

Dear Tracy,

By the time you get this letter, you'll probably know where I am. I can just picture you calling my house after you got off of work at the mall and my mom trying to answer the question "Is Anna there?" What did she say? "Oh, sorry, dear, she's at the nut house. Try back in a few months." I can't imagine she'd call it a nut house, though. She probably said something like, "emotional rehab." Maybe she didn't even tell you the truth. Shit. Did she tell you I went to a fat farm? I'll be pissed if that's what she's telling people. I'd rather be considered crazy than fat any day.

But I'm not crazy, Trace. I just can't believe I'm here. I can't believe that things got so bad that my parents sent me to a mental hospital. It's weird here, T. Right now, it's like, 10:30 at night and they have me just waiting in the middle of some hallway at one of those school desks (where the seat is connected to the desk part and there's that little book holder basket where the person behind you can stick their feet. Remember when Joe Shafton used to torment me in junior high by shaking my desk incessantly? Bastard. I finally started crying in class and the teacher let me change seats). All I have with me right now are my pillow from home (my mom packed it), and this gummed pad of paper and a suckball pencil (annoyingly without an eraser) that they oh so generously gave to me. I'm embarrassed to say that I've been crying since the moment I got here, and I think the lady at the desk is sick of hearing it. I told her you were my best friend and that I'd kill myself if they didn't let me write you a letter. The writing is helping me feel a little calmer, so that's good. I wish I could have talked to you before my parents dragged me here, but I didn't want you to freak out while you were ringing up some big thong purchase at work (do you get less commission when you sell thongs than granny underwear 'cause there's less fabric?). Sorry—I'm trying to be funny so I don't go completely insane due to the fact that I AM WRITING TO YOU FROM A LOONY BIN!!!

[Pause to note that a group of teenagers just passed me in the hallway. They were totally staring at me, so I just shoved my face into my pillow so they wouldn't see how horrid I look from all of the crying I've been doing. At least I don't wear makeup, so I don't have freakish mascara running down my cheeks.]

Lakeland Hospital. Why am I here, you ask? I don't know. I know I haven't been at school much lately, and I've been a little weird to talk to (sorry about that). I don't know what my problem is. For a while now I haven't been feeling very *normal.* Like, I can't sit through classes without getting antsy and claustrophobic and having to get up to go to the bathroom (so embarrassing). My mind starts racing and racing, and I can't concentrate on things at all. I just start thinking about how I might get a stomachache and won't be able to sit through class, and then it makes my stomach actually start to hurt and I just have to get out of there. And sometimes I worry that my stomach will make a grumbly noise, and some jerk guy will say something like, "Looks like it's time for your ten o'clock feeding, Fat Ass." I even start thinking about what would happen if (yes, you may laugh) I fart in class! Nobody forgets a class farter. I mean, I totally remember when Johnny Stran ripped one in 7th-grade history, and everyone simultaneously scooted their desks away from him—SHROOM!—so he was left alone in the middle of the classroom. I would be mortified if that happened to me. That psycho bitch therapist I saw over the summer claimed that these are called Panic Attacks, but I don't think I've ever read anything in scientific journals about fear of farting (not that I've ever actually read a scientific journal, but, whatever). Just because it supposedly has a name doesn't help the fact that I can't sit still or be near anyone. Not you, of course, but it's just nice and mellow when we hang at your house. And you wouldn't berate me if I farted in front of you (well, you might, but then I'd just remind you of that time you let out a turbo one at a slumber party while we were doing Light as a Feather, Stiff as a Board, and everyone thought it was some evil ghost fart and they dropped you).

Anyway, these panic attacks are the reasons why I'm never in class anymore. Either I ditch and hide in the bathroom, go to the nurse and lie on one of those nasty lice-proof vinyl couches and chew Pepto tablets, or convince my mom to call me in sick. That last one was getting much harder to pull off. You know how nice my mom is, but she was starting to hate lying for me. She told me she was afraid I'd never go to school again (which doesn't sound too bad to me). But she started making me feel guilty, like

I shouldn't force her to make the choice between my truancy and my happiness. And she and my dad have been fighting a lot (what else is new) because he thinks she's being too passive and should just make me go to school. I guess she kind of *is* being passive, but in this case I like it. Plus, if he wants me to go to school so badly, why doesn't *he* make me go? Not that I want him to even talk to me, but isn't that hypocritical? Mom's all worried that since it's my junior year I won't be able to get into college with all of these cuts on my record. I try to tell her that at least they're cuts from honors level classes, but that doesn't seem to help. That's why I started seeing that skag of a therapist. My mom found her by recommendation from one of her mah-jongg friends. She's kind of perverted (the therapist, not the mah-jongg friend). Everything I say she relates to sex. The other day she said I liked The Clash because, get ready for this, "Clash is a slang term for a vagina." She actually said that. What a total freak! It's not like I would listen to them for *their music* or anything. And since when is that a slang term for a vagina? She totally made that up. Plus, she's always telling me how I need to lose weight. Like I didn't know that. And how is making me feel more like shit about myself therapeutic? She analyzed this dream I had where I was pushing a shopping cart with a floppy wheel, and she said the wheel represented my "spare tire." I thought only men had spare tires. And there she is sipping on her Diet Coke the whole time. She probably goes and throws it up after each therapy session. If she doesn't sound sucky enough already, she's the one who recommended to my parents that I get hospitalized. I mean, just because I wouldn't go to school. And I want to die. But I don't remember telling her about that.

I will now describe this place to you, just in case you have to spring me and need to draw a map. To the right of where I'm sitting is an elevator with some intricate key system instead of up and down buttons, no doubt so I can't escape. In front of me is what looks like a check-in desk at a doctor's office. The hall lights are dimmed, but from what I can tell, I'm at the cross of a T-shaped series of hallways. Someone is coming. More later . . .

. . . HOURS LATER

This place sucks. I want out of here so badly. I am now sitting on a bed at the end of the hallway near the check-in counter wearing nasty blue hospital pajamas. You know how I told you I said I'd kill myself if they didn't give me this paper and pencil?

"We called your doctor," a desk lady told me.

"What doctor?"

"Your hospital psychiatrist. Until he can meet you on Monday, you're on PSI II."

Who is this "doctor" anyway? He can't even come in on a weekend to meet me to see if I'm actually suicidal or not? Probably because of his golf game, or whatever it is that those in the psychiatry business do with the overabundance of money they make *not* helping people. So now I'm on PSI II—Possible Self-Injury Level II.

Meaning, I could kill myself at any moment, so someone has to watch me constantly. I think the only thing worse is Level III, and that would have me tied up and sedated. But, oh joy, I'm lucky to only be on a bed in the hallway, instead of in a room. I miss my bedroom at home already. It was my favorite place in the whole world. I even miss the babyish clown wallpaper border my parents put up before I was born but never bothered to take down. And I totally miss my clothes because they won't give them back to me until I have proven that I won't kill myself (I'm not naked—just in a hideous blue hospital frock). How would I even do it, paper-cut my wrists until I bleed to death?

Before they gave me the PJs they made me go into a room with two big women with mustaches and thick German accents (I may be making up the mustaches and accent parts) while I took my clothes off. Thank God they didn't have to search any further than just looking *at* me, if you know what I mean. They gave me all of these psychological tests, too. I had to sit at a desk while some blond-bunned woman asked me twelve billion questions. The way she spoke to me was like I wasn't even a real person. The whole time I was crying and hugging my pillow, and she showed absolutely no sympathy. I'm sure these fools think I should be in this loony bin, with the way I'm acting. They even gave me a Rorschach test—you know, the ones where they show you blobs of ink and you have to say what comes into your head. I think I may have messed that one up, though, because each ink blob looked like the same thing to me—that piece of evil from the movie *Time Bandits.* Remember when we watched that? And there was that devil guy who exploded at the end into little pieces that all had to be collected up and contained, or else something really bad would happen? But one of his pieces (that looked like a burnt turd) was found in the little boy's toaster oven, and he kept yelling at his parents not to touch it because it's evil but they do touch it and then they blow up? Well, all of the ink blobs looked just like that piece of burnt turd evil to me, so that's what I told them.

I'm never going to get out of here, am I?

Saturday, Day 2

MORNING

I so did not sleep last night. I don't know how I could be expected to, seeing as I was lying in a bed in a hallway (which is, by the way, where I continue to sit). The night crew was two men and two women talking as loudly as possible about their personal lives. And here I was, poor little mental patient, trying to sleep not even ten feet away from their hootin' and hollerin'. I don't care that you got yourself a new weave, girl! The worst part came at 5:00 a.m. when one of the men made me sit down at the infamous desk-chair combo and took my blood. Tracy, you know how I am about needles and blood (I may have to excuse myself to go vomit as I tell this story). This fool did not know what he was doing at all. It took a million prods and pokes to find the right spot, and then it took a million hours to get the blood. They barely even acknowledged that I was scared and crying. Heartless wenches. I'm already showing some bruising on my arm. I don't even know why they took the blood! I asked the night staff if I could have my blankey for comfort. This one woman with kind, sparkly eyes said yes, but then a guy said, "No! Nuh-uh! Her record said she can't have anything yet." They think my trusty blankey could endanger my life. Oh, unlike this full-sized blanket that they have sitting on my bed! *Evil.*

I wonder what my parents would think about this. I wonder if they even think about it at all. I bet my dad is thrilled that I'm not there to cause any fights between him and my mom. And what about Mara? I never know if my sister is even aware of what's going on. It's not like she's too young to figure it out, but she's always out and about with her perfect friends and her perfect clothes and her perfect middle-school life. We used to be so close. Now she probably thinks I'm just a crazy blob of a loser.

The night shift is leaving now, and four new people are coming in. I feel like a zoo animal. No—I feel like a circus freak locked up in a cage! It's like people won't really say anything to me; they just look at me.

Maybe I should give them the finger to see what they'll do.

Yeah, like I'd ever do that.

TEN MINUTES LATER

Of course I didn't give them the finger, but I did ask if I could go to the bathroom. They got all mad and told me I'm not allowed to speak to them until they say I can. So I raised my hand, and they got all pissed and said that I'm not allowed to raise my hand; I have to stick two fingers out, not up, and I can speak when they call on me. Call on me? I'm on a bed in the middle of a hallway! This place is so weird. When they finally did "call on me," and I told them I had to go to the bathroom, a woman actually came with me! She didn't come in, but I had to leave the door open. Good thing I only had to pee. It was so awkward, though, because I started to have a panic attack and thought I had to go #2 (such a dorky way of saying "shit"), so I was in there for a long time. Fucking Irritable Bowel Syndrome. Could they think up a possibly more embarrassing name for this problem? They might as well call it "Nervous Shit Syndrome" because that's no less offensive than talking about how my bowels are irritable. All that it really means is that I get a poopy stomach when I'm nervous. How could I not be nervous locked up here?

The woman kept calling out, "Are you OK? You almost done?" What am I supposed to say to that? Hand me a magazine and stop talking to me? I wanted to ask her if she ever tried to take a crap with the door open and a stranger sitting outside. I couldn't do it, so I flushed and got back in bed. I was really anxious and felt awful, so I stuck my fingers out and asked to go to the bathroom again. "But you just went." Sigh. This scenario repeated two more times. So humiliating. I wish I were never born.

AFTER THE MORTIFYING BATHROOM SCENARIO

I got a better look at some of my fellow patients in this freak hole, and they all look pretty close to my age. They come up to the check-in desk to get pills. After they take them, the desk people look in their mouths to make sure they've swallowed. It's like something out of *The Twilight Zone.* Are they going to do that to me?

The night I got here a desk woman asked if I was on any medication, and I said, "No. Well, sometimes I take Tylenol. And Aleve for cramps." Pause. "Oh, and I've been on Lexapro for a week." I don't know why I didn't mention the antidepressant first. One would think it obvious in this sort of setting, but I haven't noticed any change in my happiness level since I started it, so it's not fresh in my mind. I know: "It takes time." But what if by the time it works I've already decided to hang myself (although definitely not the way I'd choose to off myself) or OD? What if I OD on antidepressants? Wouldn't that be ironic? It's a thought. With my luck I'd be found right away and they'd have to pump my stomach, and I'd be all full of needles and they'd make me go right back on the pills anyway. Why bother.

Maybe I haven't been as subtle as I thought I was being with the whole "thinking about death" thing. It *did* get me locked up here. I wish I could get it out of my head, but sometimes I can't. I think about dying every single morning when I wake up. Life is shit. I'm fat. I'm depressed. My own parents don't know what to do with me. I can't even sit in a classroom and hate physics tests like a normal person. I am a huge waste of life and space, and I'm tired of being alive and having to deal with it. No, I have never actually attempted suicide because I don't want to make anyone else feel bad (although it would serve my parents right for putting me in here). However, if I were to die quickly and painlessly right here, right now, I wouldn't complain at all. In fact, it would free me from ever having to complain again. Do you ever feel that way?

LATER

Holy mother of crap. The creepiest thing just happened. I was writing away when this team of men—all wearing T-shirts tucked into their elastic-waist pants—came busting out of the elevator. They looked all urgent, and I kept hearing the name "Harold." (That name has always icked me out because it was in two creepy stories I love—one where there's this ghost boy with red hair named Harold, who steals a little girl, and a Scary Story about a scarecrow named Harold that comes to life and gallops all over a roof with a stretched-out human skin. Hearing the name should have been a clue that something sinister was about to happen.) I couldn't quite catch what was going on, but I gathered that there was some guy named Harold in the Quiet Room, which is the room next door to my bed, and that the T-shirt tuckers were going to try and move him to another floor.

Nurse Man #1: Be careful, Harold's big and dangerous.

Nurse Man #2: I heard that he bit some guy's face.

Nurse Man #1: Yeah, man, that was Johnson. He transferred to Joliet Prison. Said he felt safer there.

OK, I'm totally making that dialog up. But they did say he bit someone and that he's crazy wild. So there I was in a bed next to Hannibal Lecter's room, and one of the check-in ladies told me to get up. She took me down a mystery hallway and put me into a beautiful square room filled with natural light. There was an older woman with a kind face and a boy with sandy brown hair who was maybe eight in the room with me.

"What am I doing here?" I asked them.

"This is the children's ward," the lady said. "They asked us if we would keep you here while they deal with something. You can go back to the adolescent ward when they're done." So that confirmed that everyone in my area was definitely a teenager.

The little boy worked on a jigsaw puzzle of a peaceful farm. "Where are the other kids?" I asked him, being that I assumed a "children's ward" would be stocked with children.

"I'm the only one here right now," he said, and I noticed huge, dark circles under his eyes when he looked up at me.

"Where'd everyone else go?" Because I assumed they were on a field trip or getting strip-searched or something.

"No one else has checked in for several weeks," the woman said, and as she fiddled with the kid's puzzle I pondered the fact that he was the only kid in the children's ward. All day and night he's alone, trying to fix whatever other people think is wrong with him so he can get out of the hospital and try to go back to being a normal kid. That rots.

Meanwhile, down the hall in the adolescent ward, I heard the crashing of metal trays and people yelling things like "Grab him!" and "Watch out!" I peeked my head around the corner and saw a burly giant, kind of how I pictured Lenny from *Of Mice and Men* would look if he were black, thrashing about and tossing the T-shirt tuckers off him as if he were some mutant bad guy that only a superhero could destroy. I had to stop watching when I noticed a man creeping toward Harold with a syringe. I'm guessing it was to knock him out, but I wasn't about to watch anyone being force-shot. I busied myself with the farm puzzle. Soon things got quiet. When they finally told me I could go back to my bed in the hallway (joy!), I heard some of the check-in ladies comparing notes:

"Oh, man, I think I got some blood on my sleeve."

"That's just chocolate."

"You know I'm allergic to chocolate."

"And you know that ain't Harold's blood." They laughed, so I think they were kidding.

This place is supposed to make me feel better?

SATURDAY AFTERNOON

Here I am, back at the connect-o desk. They tried to feed me earlier with a cliché pile of mushy hospital food in a segregated plastic tray, but I didn't eat. I couldn't eat. Never in my life have I skipped a meal, but being trapped here has magically disintegrated my will to chow down. Who knows? Maybe I can start the new Mental Hospital Diet. "Lose your sanity and twenty pounds!" That's the weird thing: I'm supposed to be here to get better, right? So I can go to class and not be depressed, right? But so far no one has even offered to introduce themselves to me. Soon after the Harold incident I started crying again uncontrollably.

"Please let me call my parents!" I yelled and pleaded with the check-in lady. "They made a mistake. I'm not supposed to be here! There's nothing wrong with me! I need to go home!" It was kind of embarrassing. I don't think I have ever full-on yelled at someone other than my sister before, but I felt so desperate and I hadn't gotten in trouble yet so I thought I'd go for it. It was like the lady was immune to being screamed at. She ignored me for about ten minutes, and then said that my doctor would be here on Monday and he would let me know what's going on. "If you're good," she said, "we can try to get him on the phone so you can get off of PSI II and into your own room." If I'm good? Does that mean they think I'm bad? I've never been bad a day in my life. Are they pissed that I needed to spend so much time in the bathroom? That I raised my hand? Maybe it was the yelling. Shit. I hope I didn't screw up getting my own room. What if I have to sleep in the hall forever?

In more promising hallway news, there is a rather hot boy sitting at a desk down the hall who keeps giving me evil looks.

LATER

I can't believe I have been here less than twenty-four hours. This is so pointless, and I feel gross because I'm sitting in the middle of a hallway with paper-thin pajamas on, and I'm not wearing a bra. In real life, I wouldn't dare leave the house with my C cups flopping all over the place, but I would also never sit at a desk in the middle of a hallway in pajamas. Come to think of it, I wouldn't normally wear a bra under my pajamas (unlike Carrie on *Sex and the City.* Is she *that* fashion-conscious that she has to look stylishly trashy in bed when no one can even see her?). My only motivation to put my bra on is the kind-of-hot-but-kind-of-not guy sitting down the hall. He, too, has the black circles under his eyes (and Ramones-y pale skin). As he has been writing on his desk this whole time (the desk, mind you, not paper *on* the desk), I know he is left-handed (always a turn-on). He has short, dark hair that in these last few hours he has managed to twist into tiny wanna-be dreadlocks (white guys with dreads—always a turnoff). Anytime I look at him he curls his lip and blows out through his mouth in that "yeah, right" way I'm so used to seeing from the opposite sex. Maybe he'd change his mind if I put my bra on.

Desk Lady told me that she talked to my "doctor" and that

he'll come in tomorrow to see if I'm ready for PSI I. Remember at summer camp when we were little and we had to take swim tests, and each time we passed we moved up to a more advanced fish name? As if a tuna swims better than a chub. I feel excited like that, like tomorrow I'm going to show them that I, too, can do the breaststroke! But instead of a nice certificate and Free Swim privileges, I'll just get to stop sleeping on a bed in a hallway. And hopefully they'll give me my bra back (and then I can really do the breaststroke! Ha! Get it?). But still no blankey . . .

P.S. If anyone asks, say I'm sick.

Day 3 Sunday! Sunday! Sunday!

Ah, Tracy, this is the life. I have my own room (door still open), my own bed (foam mattress, so I don't break it open and pull out the springs in order to harm myself or others), and a view of the city (through a thick escape-proof screen). My doctor was an asshole when I met with him this morning, and will here on out be referred to as "Dr. Asshole." (In print only. I don't want him to put me back on PSI II.) He looked alarmingly similar to the psychiatrist on *The Simpsons*—short, round glasses, and a bald yarmulke on the top of his head. He wore a brown suit today, the kind where the fabric looks all knotty and could use one of those electric lint-ball removers (I have always wanted one of those). He has a little office here with his comfy chair and a nasty, sunken couch for the patients to lie on. The first thing I did when he closed the office door was start crying and begging him to let me call my parents. "Shut up, and stop being such a baby," he reprimanded. Is it legal for him to talk to me like that? I told him I haven't eaten anything since I got here. "Isn't that a sign that I'm not adjusting and should be sent home?" I prodded. His response was, "You could stand to lose a few pounds, couldn't you?" What a dick!

Dr. A-Bomb flipped through what I assumed to be my chart and said, "I see you recently started on Lexapro. How's that going for you?"

I wanted to say that it obviously wasn't going so well, seeing as I was recently admitted to a mental hospital. Instead I said, "I don't know. I don't feel any different."

"It usually takes several weeks for the meds to kick in." Then he surprised me with, "Do you still want to kill yourself?"

I never really want to kill myself; I just want to die some kind of quick, painless death to put me out of my misery. "No," was my answer.

"Fine," he told me, all blasé. "You're on PSI I now. Go sit in your room."

"Can I have my bra back?" I asked him, seeing as I'd already hit rock bottom on the humiliation ladder, what with my weepy outburst and my unsolicited weight loss counseling.

"I'll see what I can do."

Even though he was kind of a turd sticker, I liked that he didn't feed me any flaky analytical bullshit. He still gets the Asshole name, though.

At least I have my own room now. It's actually the room right next door to the Quiet Room and my old hallway bed. There's a second bed in here, so I may have a roommate at some point. A lady at the check-in desk said that there are only two other girls on the floor right now (they refer to the adolescent ward as "the floor." I'm really getting hip to the lingo). The next girl that arrives will be mine—my roommate, that is. But I was here first, so it's my turf.

A room description: The room has two desks and two nightstands. There's a scary brown closet near the window that has lots and lots of shelves. I pray I won't be here long enough to have the need to fill any of them.

As of now, they still won't let me have any of the things I packed from home. A short list of crap I brought but cannot have:

1. That good-luck frog pin you gave me when you went on that cruise to the Bahamas and made out with that metalhead guy whose last name sounded like a cough syrup brand
2. Two Ramones T-shirts
3. One Green Day T-shirt, pre-sellout
4. Earplugs for sleeping
5. My trusty blankey (also for sleeping)
6. An 8 × 10 glossy picture of Dee Dee Ramone rockin' out
7. Various mismatching clothes that I grabbed last minute

⑧ My iPod—God, I wish I could just plug myself into my headphones, close my eyes, and forget where I am completely

Back to the room description: The walls are covered with a sticky, slightly padded substance in soothing pastel pinks and blues so I won't want to kill myself. Remember when we learned about that black bridge in sociology class? People kept jumping off of it, so they painted it powder blue. I bet the only reason that brought the suicide numbers down is the humiliating thought of having someone say, "Steve killed himself by jumping off a powder blue bridge." They're thinking the walls will lull me into a calmed state?

My room is connected to the other girls' room by a bathroom. One door to the bathroom is on my side, the other on theirs. There's no lock on the door, so we're supposed to knock before we go in. I'm guessing it's so no one gets locked in and tries to drown themselves in the toilet. How is anyone supposed to poop when someone might just bust in during the process? This place is going to make me so constipated.

EVENING

Joy! I've been so "good" that they're going to let me join in on the Sunday night movie! "You can go to the Sunday night movie in the Day Room." That's what the desk lady said. Am I supposed to know what that means? Should I stick my two fingers out while I watch it? Apparently, every Sunday night they show a movie, and the "Day Room" is a room where all the kids go to watch it. I'll let you know how that goes—actual socializing with other loony kids! And, good news, I got my bra back, so I can attend the screening in style. Stay tuned . . .

LATER

Well, my evening was less than dramatic. We watched the first (or is it fourth?) *Star Wars*. I sat in the back of the room, in a chair behind everyone else (so no one even got to see my bra-supported breasts). The Day Room was long, with a twenty-inch TV against one wall about eighty miles away from where I was sitting. The chairs in the room were booger green and vomit brown faux leather that made highly embarrassing fart noises when anyone sat, moved, or got off of them. There were maybe fifteen kids watching the flick (I have always vowed to use the word "flick" more), but by the time I strutted my stuff on the red carpet (actually paisley and pukey) the room was dark and I couldn't see their faces. We were given Dixie cups filled with popcorn, and I ate some. Does that count as eating? Or can I still claim that I haven't eaten here? It really only amounted to six kernels of popcorn anyway.

The night crew woman with the shiny eyes, whom I will now call "Sparkle" (even though it makes her sound like a My Little Pony) shuffled me back to my room. She told me to get excited because tomorrow I will get a shower and will go to my first Community meeting. I have no idea what that means, but it sounds awfully cult-ish. I'll let you know how it goes. They're turning out the lights now. Good night.

EXTRA! EXTRA! BREAKING LATE-NIGHT NEWS!

I got my blankey! Sparkle brought it in! I feel like jumping up and doing a celebratory Snoopy dance! Oh, trusty blankey. You are my true friend.

Monday, Day 4

MORNING

I totally did not sleep last night. I could hear every single inane conversation the night crew was having AGAIN. So much for having walls. Plus, all night my mind was racing racing racing about every little lame thing: Would being here stop me from getting into college? Do I even want to go to college? Do my teachers know where I am? Are they going to think I'm a total psycho when I get back to school? Will I ever go back to school? Will I be here until I'm fifty, in the same pajamas and bra? At least I can go to the bathroom by myself.

LUNCHTIME

I was actually busy all morning. First I had a shower. At about 6:30 a.m., a desk lady escorted me and the two other girls to the shower room. I had envisioned a big room with shower heads popping out of the walls and having to shower as fast as possible while armed guards marched back and forth. It wasn't nearly that bad; we at least had our own private shower stalls. We only got ten minutes from the time we stepped out of our bedrooms to the second we stepped back in. I had to wash my hair really fast, which almost makes me wish that my hair wasn't so long. I got a quick glimpse of the other girls as I squished my clothes on. One was a grungy white girl with hair that looked like a bowl, and the other was a petite black girl who I thought looked nice until she flipped me the bird. Nobody said anything during the whole shower experience, but I couldn't tell if that was because they didn't want to waste any of their precious ten minutes on chatting or if we weren't allowed to talk because of some rule. Or maybe they were just bitches. When I got back to my room there was a fresh hospital PJ ensemble waiting for me. It's amazing how something can be blue and yet absolutely colorless. I wonder when I'll get my clothes back.

After I changed (which didn't even feel like changing, since I was just putting on pajamas again), I lay down on top of my bedspread. That's what I always like to do at home. I reserve going under the sheets only for sleeping; that way, they stay cold and fresh. I hope that doesn't sound crazy. I have this fear that people are reading my mail, looking for signs of lunacy.

Kind of strange, but I haven't had a bad panic attack since the phantom poo incident two days ago. I feel more dazed than panicked, and no one's really paying much attention to me. As long as I'm left alone in my room, there's not much fear of pooping or farting. God, I sound gross. Of course those aren't my only fears, but if no one's around to hear (or smell!) then it's one thing less to worry about. Not going to school takes a mega worry away, but now I'm scared about having a freakout during "Community." I wish I knew how long it will last. Sometimes that makes me feel better, knowing there's an end in sight.

In other news, I finally ate a meal. They brought a tray with Cap'n Crunch and some orange juice to my room. I've never had Cap'n Crunch before. My mom won't buy it because she thinks we should all start our day the healthy bran way. I may have started my day with bran, but the moment I got to school I headed straight to the vending machines and bought myself some Little Debbie Zebra Cakes. They do say you should eat a balanced breakfast, and I felt the creamy goodness of the Zebra Cakes balanced out the paperlike quality of the bran quite nicely. Cap'n Crunch isn't exactly a Zebra Cake, but it is pretty good, despite the strange, pasty texture. And I can't deny the sugar buzz. I topped it off with OJ in a little plastic cup with a peel-back foil lid. It was obviously not anywhere near fresh-squeezed, and it burnt my throat.

After breakfast they told me to get ready to go to Community. I still didn't know what it was, but I knew I'd probably be seeing the other kids and wanted to look somewhat decent. I looked in the wavy plastic bathroom mirror and couldn't believe how nasty I looked. My hair was kind of ratty because there was no time to condition it (and I can't comb my curls or they frizz). My face looked all jaundice-y, and I had purple puffs underneath my eyes. So much for my stunning debut. I took two deep breaths and followed one of the desk people down the hall.

Community turned out to be a group meeting of sorts. The grand ol' Day Room had its fart chairs set up in a circle, and each chair had a kid perched on it. I sat down on a green chair, let it rip, and chuckled to myself as I looked around to see if anyone else thought it funny. No one did. I glanced up at a few people, but no one looked at me. I must have really looked like ass, especially because I was the only one wearing hospital pajamas. I wonder if they thought I was crazy.

There were about fifteen teenagers, mostly boys, and two adults leading the meeting: One was a greasy-looking guy with a mustache (the words "greasy" and "mustache" should always appear together in a sentence) named Eugene, and the other was a larger woman with a South Side accent named Bettina. Bettina started the meeting by announcing "Restrictions." Two boys stuck their fingers out (two-finger style, out, not up). Bettina called, "Phil," and this short guy, looking exactly like a miniature Shaggy from *Scooby-Doo*, stood up.

"I got a one-hour room restriction for telling Matt O. he's a dickhead." The adults nodded, as if this were standard stuff. I wanted to laugh, but, of course, no one else was smiling.

Bettina called out, "Troy," and the hottie from the hallway stood up.

"I'm still on hall restriction for hitting Benny in the head with a chair." Can you believe that? I was totally freaked out at the prospect of him being violent, and yet I still found myself curiously attracted to him, twisty dreads and all.

"Confrontations," Eugene announced. He spoke as if he had a bubble in his throat. The girl who gave me the finger in the shower (whoa—that sounds raunchy!) stuck out her hand. "Tanya." When she stood up I got a better look at her than the showers allowed. Tanya was cute and petite—all perfectly fitting clothes and a teeny waist. I wondered if her obnoxiously bitchy air made her less attractive to guys, or if they even care about personalities at all.

Tanya turned to Bowlhead from the showers and said, "Jolene, I am mad that you kept me up all night snorin' like my wrinkly ol' bulldog, Dexter." I noticed a couple of guys holding in smiles (so at least we know their faces hadn't been tampered with to prevent smiling).

"Tanya," Eugene said, shaking his head. "You do that same confrontation every day. Do you think I'm gonna give you points for that? You do that again, and I'm gonna give you a restriction." Tanya flared her nostrils and sighed out of them like a bull.

"Apologies." Jolene and a rather cute boy that I hadn't noticed before stuck their fingers out. "Jolene." Bettina called on her, and she stood, placing her hands stiffly against her sides. Jolene, sorry to say, was pretty homely. The bowl haircut was just the icing on her stylish-less cake. She was wearing leggings, which I guess are making a comeback (damn everyone to hell for that), but she had on a tight, generic Mickey Mouse T-shirt OVER a pink, poofy-sleeved blouse. I don't know if she looked worse than I did, but it made me feel a little better.

"Tanya, I just want to say that I'm really sorry for keeping you awake. But tomorrow's my release day, so you can just suck it, bitch." Jolene looked smugly at Tanya.

"That's a one-hour room restriction, Jolene." Eugene took notes as he said this. "And you can write an apology letter while you're in there."

"Like I give a shit. I'm out of here." Then she flashed this faux-homey peace sign.

Eugene moved on to the newly discovered cutie. "Justin." Justin stood up with his hands in his pockets, looking remarkably tall even with the standard cute-boy slouch. His hair was straight and brown, and the strands in front of his face were just long enough to settle on his eyelashes. His hair bounced each time he blinked. "Matt O., I want to apologize for losing your pencil." And then he sat, head down, hair blocking my view of his sweet face. He lost a pencil. I'm sure whatever he was doing with that pencil must have been very important, or Matt O., whoever he is, would have his pencil back! Perhaps he was sketching a picture of a pet from long ago, or writing a poem about the loneliness of the waning moon. Or maybe he was trying to stab other patients with it. . . . Whatever it was for, I'm sure he had a good reason for losing it. It does kind of make me wonder, though, what kind of guy Matt O. is if he needed an apology for losing his pencil. Wow, Justin is quite lovely.

"Appreciation." Eugene announced this, and five people stood up. I won't bore you with the lame details, but the appreciations all went something like this: "(Insert crazy teenager's name here), I appreciated (choose one) eating dinner with you/talking with you at lunch/that joke you told. . . ." They all seemed like pretty bland things to be appreciated for, so maybe that's a good indication of things to come here.

When Appreciation was over, the staff selectively chose people to excuse from the meeting. It was like in first grade when the teacher would look around the room and let the people who were being good go out to recess first. I was the baddy because I didn't get to go until everyone else had left. Actually, I think it was because I was the only person in the room with an escort. Nobody looked at me as they passed: Anna the Dog-faced Girl.

BORING IN-ROOM TIME, STILL MONDAY

They obviously don't trust that we will not try to jump out our windows because they are covered up with this impossibly thick wire screen. My view is very city: dirty-looking, nondescript buildings, many with yellow pieces of laundry hanging from the windows. Right across the street appears to be some sort of junky hotel because cars keep pulling up under what looks like a check-in awning. In the parking lot there are two really cool old cars, one pink and one powder blue (God, do you think the hospital placed them there to soothe us as we look out our windows?). They kind of look space-age, like they're from a

1950s movie that's supposed to take place in the distant future but everything still looks funky and retro. Maybe there are men from the future staying at the junky hotel! I will try to send them a message of peace with my light switch.

THINKING . . .

I just realized that I didn't have a panic attack in Community. I wonder why. Probably because I was so focused on all of the high drama and cute boys that I forgot to have one. Or maybe the antidepressants are kicking in (doubtful). Or maybe they're pumping some sort of antidepressant gases through the ventilation system here.

AFTERNOON

I'm back in the hallway at a desk. They said it was too depressing for me to be sitting in my room alone all day. The good news is that tomorrow I get to meet with Doc Asshole about getting off of PSI I and getting my clothes back! Plus, Troy the dreadlocked wonder not only leered at me today—he gave me the finger!

LATE

What the hell is with this place? I have no clue what I'm doing here, and everyone acts like I'm supposed to just know about everything that's going on! They told me to come into the hall with my pillow, so I went out there and started to ask what was going on. They SHHHSHed me all obnoxiously, so I just stood there, arms full of pillow. Then all of the guys walked by me in a line, and I was totally excited because cute boy Justin LOOKED at me, even though I'm in gross hospital PJs, but then some hag at the check-in desk told me to stop smiling. I don't get it. They want me not to be depressed, yet a person, let alone the cutest guy here, looked at me for the first time and they tell me not to smile.

Tanya and Jolene came out of their room with pillows, and a woman who came on duty while I was waiting in the hall whispered to follow her. Her name tag said "Flora," which was appropriate, as she had on a flowery dress and had a flowery voice. Flora led us down the hallway, where I normally sit at the desk, into a small room with all of the lights off. Of course I'm thinking here's where the cultish crap begins, but then she popped in a James Taylor tape. Isn't that song "Fire and Rain" about a girl who dies in a plane crash and James wanting to kill himself because of it? Is that appropriate to play in a mental hospital? Maybe it's *too* appropriate. Maybe there's an entire soundtrack that mental hospitals pay for, to include songs such as Madonna's "Crazy for You" and "Crazy" by Gnarls Barkley. God, I can think of a million songs with "crazy" in the title. I'll have to boycott them if I ever get out of here.

I watched Tanya and Jolene put their pillows on the floor and lie down. I took my cue from them, dropped my pillow, and began to hunker down onto the floor, but just as I was about to get comfortable Flora stopped me. "This is Relaxation. We do not drop our pillows during Relaxation. You need to go back to your room now." Huh? Did I just get in trouble for DROPPING MY PILLOW? I have no clue. How *would* I know? How will I ever know if I'm not allowed to talk to anybody or smile at anybody or condition my hair, for that matter?! I feel like there should be circus music blaring *do do doodle loodle do do doodle* and a barker shouting, "Come look at the freaks!"

If only I had some of my own music to soothe me to sleep. It would be so great if I could somehow teleport my stereo from home into my room here. I know the sound is really crappy, since I've had it since 7th grade, but I miss it! I even miss the scratch-and-sniff stickers I covered it with to make it look cooler. I'm not sure that the stickers ever achieved the cool look I was going for, but at least it smelled pretty good.

Tuesday, Day 5

Dear Tracy,

Hurray! Hurray! They're going to give me my clothes back today! Now I can be a lunatic *in style*. I met with Dr. Asshole today, and he took me off PSI I and put me on Level 0. What that means is that now that I'm not threatening to kill myself, I can earn points by hitting people in the head with chairs and stealing pencils! Actually, I may lose points for that, but live and learn! The goal here is to obtain points by being a good girl, i.e.: doing what I'm told, making an obvious effort to fix what is supposedly wrong with me, and getting along with others. When these points add up, I get onto higher levels, which allow me exciting new privileges, like going to the cafeteria to eat! Watching one half hour of TV per day! And if I'm extra good I may win up to $25,000 at Plinko! All Plinkos aside, it doesn't sound very hard. It's not like I'll be throwing chairs or stealing pencils or anything bad like that. I hate getting in trouble.

Doc A-Hole said that most of the therapy I have to do here is group work, but I'll meet with him about once a week. It's so weird that they just hook me up with some random guy shrink and I'm expected to be OK with that. What if I don't want to tell him anything? I'm starting to get a stomachache.

LATER

Tragedy strikes! I so was not thinking when I packed my clothes to come here. Why did my mom let me leave home without my red Converse All Stars? Now I'm stuck in a very chilly mental hospital forced to wear the shoes I had on when I got here—flip-flops—with socks! I recognize that some folks in the world think the whole socks and sandals bit is cool, but to me it equals white people with hemp hoodies listening to Phish and stinking up the hallways at school with patchouli. This is so not me. I would much rather have my comfy, worn-in, hole in the right toe, low-top red Converse All Stars. I noticed that Justin had black Chucks. I thought maybe if I had my Chucks here that we could bond over our choice in footwear, but nooooo. He's going to think I'm a dork and won't ever look at me again, and I'll become an old maid and live in this mental hospital for the rest of my life without getting a date. What if?

AFTERNOON

I just had my first group therapy session. The floor is divided into two groups, A and B. I don't quite know how they choose which kid goes into which group, but I'm in B. Because you are dying to know, Justin is not in Group B. Tanya, however, *is* in Group B, which sucks because she is a royal bitch who gives me an "eat shit" look every time I glance her way. I'd try to look tough, but I don't want her to kick my ass. I've never even been close to having my ass kicked, but I'd like to believe that if it ever happened I would have some sort of built-in kung fu abilities that would automatically activate. And there's always our self-defense training from gym class: Always go for the eyes, nose, and throat. (I still think it's totally ironic that while the girls were learning self-defense in gym class, the guys were in a different room learning wrestling.) Thankfully, Tanya spent most of Group staring at the floor, trying not to have to speak to anyone.

We had Group in the Day Room, where we actually got to sit in nonfarting chairs that were placed in a circle. Eugene led Group, and because it was my first time, everyone had to do a little introduction of themselves. Very Alcoholics Anonymous. It was about time someone actually told me something. Not that anything anyone said was very informative. I had to go first, which I guess was good because then I could relax a little and hear what everyone else had to say.

"I'm Anna Bloom. I'm sixteen. I have a younger sister, Mara. I like to listen to music, mostly punk. I'm teaching myself to play the bass. The Cap'n Crunch here is pretty good." That got some light chuckles. I thought I was finished, but Eugene looked at me to continue. "That's it," I said.

"And why are you here?"

"I don't know," I shrugged. "I guess because I stopped going to school." And that's when the tears started. Embarrassed, I didn't want to say anything more. I simpered through the entire hour as I listened to everyone else's stories.

Victor, a short African-American guy, seemed pretty funny, although he's definitely a lot more city than I am (which probably isn't saying much, as I am a card-carrying suburbanite). He said he was here "Because they didn't like the fact that I was selling drugs in school. But I told them it was the only way to pay for my mom's cancer treatment. They were soft on me and sent me here instead of jail." I wonder who sells drugs at our school. I wonder if they would sell them to me.

Unfortunately, Phil/Shaggy is in my group. He has a lewd (funny word!) way of looking around at people that makes me want to wash my hands. Someone needs to hose this freak down 'cause the way he introduced himself was by saying, "I'm sure glad we're getting some more ladies on this floor." I don't care if guys never give me that kind of attention; I do NOT want it from the likes of him.

"And why are you here?" asked Eugene.

"Oh, you know, I got myself in a little trouble. You might say I was playing with fire." He looked at me out of the corner of his eye.

"And you might say that he set some girl's house on fire 'cause she wouldn't go out with him," explained Victor.

Matt O. (the soul without a pencil) sat next to me (and was rather ripe in the b.o. department). He's a sweet-faced guy who has apparently been in this place for six months. Six months! I hope that's not the norm. He never actually said how he got here in the first place. All he said was, "I've been here for six months, and now they've got me on a new plan that lets me eat whatever I want and go to the Quiet Room whenever I want. My doc says we needed to try something different."

After six months, maybe it doesn't matter why he's here in the first place. It's like, after you're here for so long, whatever happened in real life probably floated away. For some of these people, that's not such a bad thing. Take Colby (like the cheese), also a member of Group B. He's a scrawny and shy kid who apparently has problems hearing voices. I mean, he doesn't actually have problems hearing voices. He hears them fine. They just happen to be inside of his head. He claims they started jabbering after he began playing Dungeons and Dragons with his older brother. What is the deal with people and role-playing games? You and I have played a little, Trace, and we know that there is nothing about it that would make you hear voices or kill people or channel the underworld. Plus, who blames Dungeons and Dragons for evildoing anymore? That's so '80s. Aren't we supposed to blame violence on TV or video games? Colby does seem kind of peculiar, though, so who knows. Sean, a member of Group B with a nasty scum-stache ("nasty" may be substituted for "greasy" when discussing mustaches), said that he would lend Colby one of his rosaries to protect him. I have two things to say about that: 1. How is a rosary going to protect Colby from the wrath of a game? and 2. *One* of his rosaries? Sean's story sounded exactly like the stereotypical rebel character in any teen movie (aside from the rosary deal): He was kicked out of school, sent to boarding school, escaped and ran away, got caught, and was sent here. He nervously gnawed on his fingers the whole time we had Group, and I swear I could see little droplets of blood.

As we rounded the circle, the last person to introduce himself was Bobby. In a way he reminded me of Mara. He said that he was only twelve years old, but he was here because he got into a lot of fights with his brother. When Eugene asked him to elaborate, Bobby said, "I hurt him." That reminded me of one time when Mara and I were wrestling. She started to pull my hair, I pulled hers back, and then she kicked me in the face. I had a black eye for weeks which showed up in my 7th-grade yearbook picture. Fighting with siblings is normal. Everyone here looked relatively normal to me or, at least, not crazy, which is more than I can say about myself. Nobody else cried at all. They probably think I'm a freak and should be locked up in a ward with Harold. I'm sure the socks and sandals didn't help my case.

TUESDAY AFT

As I waited around in my room with nothing to do (I'm not bad enough to be punished somewhere, and I'm not good enough to be doing anything else), I decided to do some decorating. I've been saving the foil lids from my juices, and I used the sticky power of the wall covering to create a design on the wall. It looks kind of cool, and gives the wall a juicy fragrance. Until it molds, that is. Too bad I don't have that hilarious 'N Sync poster that you and I fake autographed in grade school with "Anna, I'd like to be 'N Sync with you! Signed, Lance Bass." That would spice this place up, although it would also mean I'd have to look at their deranged '90s hairstyles.

Future Cars from the Past Update: Either whoever owns the cars has moved them while I wasn't looking and then put them back in the same spots, or the cars have not moved. Mysterioso.

PRE-DINNER

Dear Tracy,

By some amazing stroke of luck, I have skipped Level I and am now a rockin' Level 2 girl. Apparently all of my crying during

Group gave me a butt-load of bonus points, so now I can go down to the cafeteria to eat! Which means two things: I may find something I want to eat besides Cap'n Crunch, and I hopefully get to see Justin! I'll report back after dinner.

POST-DINNER

Dinner was kind of cool. Since Jolene was released today and Tanya was on Restriction, I was the only girl on the floor allowed to go down to the cafeteria. Normally, boys and girls are taken on two separate elevator trips to prevent touch-age, but lazy-ass Eugene decided I wasn't trouble enough for a second trip.

There I was in an elevator full of boys, and for the first time in my life I felt kind of attractive (even with the socks and sandals). When Eugene wasn't looking, boys would actually sneak smiles at me! Victor, the reformed drug dealer, was standing next to me, and I swear he kept touching his arm to mine on purpose. Kinky.

Once we got into the cafeteria we were allowed to talk to each other. It made everyone else seem a lot more normal, so hopefully I seemed like more than a pale, dumpy, crying girl with dark circles under her eyes wearing flip-flops with socks. The cafeteria was just like any cafeteria, except that instead of jocks at one table and Goths at another, there were drooly old people at one table and people talking to themselves at another. They must be on other floors, thank god, because they were creepy. Is that mean? I guess even in the world of crazy there's a coolness scale.

Since Matt O. has been here the longest and we are in Group together, I asked him what was good in the cafeteria. "Nothing," he answered with a small smile. It was a predictable TV show moment. Justin was a couple of people behind me in line, and I glanced back at him a few times while everyone talked. He was pretty quiet, but he smiled enough that he looked like a friendly guy. He ordered a hamburger, Tater Tots, and red Jell-O. (I have to question the Jell-O choice. It seems so hospital cliché. The only time I'll ever eat Jell-O is if I have puked and I can't stomach anything else.) I had a little nervous stomachache, but I didn't want to seem odd, so I ordered a cheeseburger and Tater Tots and took a fruit punch that was in the same type of tin-lid cup as the OJ. Then I was worried that I looked like a pig for ordering so much food. Like they were thinking, "No wonder she looks like that. Look at all that shit she eats." But I couldn't eat most of it anyway. I usually do most of my eating alone. Unless I'm put back in my room again, that doesn't seem like it's going to be an option here.

Since there were less than ten of us (due to all of the people that remained upstairs on Restriction), we all sat at the same table. It was the kind that has individual circle seats attached, ensuring that everyone has their own equal amount of butt space. The cafeteria was far better lit than our floor upstairs. It made me feel more awake than I've felt in days. I was getting tired of being so mopey. Those guys were talking to me and laughing, and they didn't make any references to all of my crying and carrying on from the past few days. It was almost like our school lunches of yore.

Bobby sat on one side of me, and Victor sat on the other side. Matt O. was across from me, with Justin on his left side. They seemed to be friends, despite the nasty "pencil incident." They included me in their conversation, so I felt brave enough to ask, "Why do they call you 'Matt O.'?"

"Matt's such a common name that every few weeks or so a new Matt comes in. It gets too confusing, so they added the O. from my last name. They never bother to take it away when there isn't another Matt here."

"Hmmm. Sounds kind of rock star-ish." I smiled.

"Yeah, like Madonna," Bobby chided.

Everyone laughed like this was the funniest thing in the world. Bobby's so cute and young, like a cuddly team mascot.

There weren't any dinner convos about the real world; we mostly talked about stuff going on inside the hospital. Kind of weird. They *did* cue me in on a bunch of rules and tricks of the mental hospital trade. Following is a selection of the weirdest:

★ You must not drop your pillow in Relaxation. Set it down gently, lie on the floor, and try to be lulled into boredom by the soothing sounds of James Taylor.

✱ The easiest way to get points is to give an Appreciation at Community. That way you don't get anyone mad, and you make yourself look good by saying nice things.

☺ Smiling will get you into trouble because an adult will think you are either planning something against them or making fun of them. Hence, no one ever smiled back at me.

✱ Never cross your arms because it may be construed as a confrontation or gang-related. (I'm one of the founders of the Socks and Sandals Gang. Watch your back!)

✱ We go to "school" for a couple of hours each day. This is the best time to "mess around" because there are only two teachers and there are lots of little rooms that the kids are spread out in. I'm not sure if "mess around" meant goof off or something else. Seeing as I was the only female at the table, I didn't want to ask.

The two most important rules, according to the boys:

✱ No relationships. Meaning, no one is allowed to become boyfriend and girlfriend, or boyfriend and boyfriend, or girlfriend and girlfriend. This is because we are supposed to be working on our problems, not making new ones.

✱ No touching. At all. No shaking hands, no touching shoulders, not even touching arms in the elevator.

At the dinner table, everyone looked stiff as they sat next to each other. I think it's pretty cold not to be able to feel the warmth and texture of another person's skin, even if it's not in a sexual way. Like when Mara leans her head on my shoulder on long car trips. I can't imagine what it must be like for Matt O., who hasn't had any human contact for six months. Trace, try walking down the halls at school without touching someone for an entire day. It makes you walk differently, doesn't it? I feel stiffer already.

They also told me to, from now on, refer to Lakeland as Lake Shit. Sounds about right.

Wednesday, Day 6

Tracy!

It's a bright, bright, bright sunshiny day! (Gross! I hate that song!) First thing in the morning, a worker came into my room with a bag of clothes that my parents dropped off last night (I will not yet get into how disturbing it is that my parents were here last night and *didn't visit me*), and I got my Chucks back! Not to mention my favorite soft jeans with the red stitching around the bottoms and my black Ramones T-shirt with the bleach stains from when we tried to highlight your hair. I put the shirt on, and now I can at least feel a little more like myself.

Before I tell you about the even *cooler* thing that happened at Community, I am going to rant about my parents. Prepare yourself.

WHAT THE HELL?! How could they be here and not come see me? How could they come and bring me more clothes, meaning they're not going to get me out of here anytime soon, and not talk to me about it? I feel so betrayed. Like they trusted all of these adults who don't know anything about me and who, of course, think I'm crazy because they saw me screaming and crying and because I said I wanted to kill myself (who doesn't think that from time to time?), and they didn't even bother to talk to me about how I haven't been eating and how my psychiatrist is a dickhead and how I got into trouble for dropping my stupid pillow! How is it that they manage to go to work every day? The part that gets me is that my dad can go to work and be with all of his students' bullshit, but he can't handle dealing with mine? And what is my mom telling her customers at the knit shop? I know they gossip and brag about their kids all of the time. Is she pretending nothing's wrong, as usual? I almost don't want to go home now, so I don't have to be with those traitors. But I still want to 'cause I miss you. ☺ Go teepee my parents' house tonight, will you?

Now for the cool news: Matt O. stood up at Appreciation and said, "Anna, I appreciated eating dinner with you last night." Someone enjoyed my presence! Albeit, not the right someone, but I felt like I kind of fit in. I thought about standing up and saying, "Justin, I appreciate your hotness," but I didn't think I'd get any points for that. I also noticed Justin looking at my Chucks possibly thinking that we were soul mates for wearing the same shoes. (Or should I say *sole* mates?) If only I had my retired Converse collection here. I could be irresistible in my green

Chucks with the duct-taped bottoms. Although, if I recall, they do have a distinctive scent. Or, should I say, di*stink*tive. I'm so punny today!

LATER IN THE DAY

Guess what—I've got a roommate! She calls herself Sandy. (Ever notice how in other languages you introduce yourself by saying "I call myself . . . ," like "Me llamo Lupita"? I am bringing that into the English language. I call myself "Bored Person.") Sandy is from Joliet (the city on the South Side with both a casino and a jail!). She's teeny but has huge, blond, fried hair. Already she has plastered twenty-six pictures of her buff boyfriend up around her desk. She hasn't said much, but it doesn't strike me as bitchiness as much as sadness and confusion.

"I don't know. I guess it's 'cause I don't get along with my parents," she tried to explain to me how she got here. "I ran away to live with my grandparents, my parents didn't like it, came to get me, and now I'm here."

It seems more and more evident that parents don't know what to do with their kids, so they just pawn them off on morons who don't know anything about their kids and get paid a lot of money to enforce lame rules like no pillow dropping. I wonder if my parents checked this place out before they brought me, or if they just trusted that this place would "fix" me and they could feel OK about themselves because I'm being "taken care of," when really they should feel like shit for abandoning me.

Sandy was smart enough not to tell the staff that she was contemplating suicide, so she's wearing her own clothes. Unfortunately, she seems to be stuck in some sort of small-town '90s time warp of big hair, stone-washed overalls, and white leather Keds. At least she hasn't given me the finger.

After briefing Sandy on the rules, I went down to dinner. Sandy is only a Level I; therefore she ate in our room.

I am starting to look forward to the elevator rides. There's something very forbidden about touching someone's arm "by accident" when there's no touching allowed. Unfortunately, I am always next to Eugene on one side and Victor on the other. So far no Justin contact, but I'll be sure to keep you up to date on any pertinent arm-touching occurrences in the future.

Dinner was once again kind of fun, in the "I'm-still-trapped-in-a-mental-hospital-and-eating-shitty-food-with-a-bunch-of-guys-I-barely-know" kind of way.

Justin complimented my Ramones shirt in the food line. "You like the Ramones?" I asked, too eagerly.

"Well, I used to." It was his turn to order food and then my turn, and by the time we got to the table that conversation was gone, and the buzz was all about Sandy.

"Is she hot?" drooled Phil/Shaggy. He's sick. He looks like a hyena, all desperate and greedy. He even laughs like a hyena! I can picture him doing that little prancy pacing that hyenas do while they wait to feed off of someone else's kill. I told him that Sandy was cute and that she has a very large boyfriend back home.

"Well, he ain't here."

"As if that would make your chances any better," I retorted. I wish I could have thought of something spunkier, but I've never been one for classic comeback lines. Still, I got some laughs. Even my not-so-funny lines are funny here in Bummerville.

I noticed that Justin was eating with his left hand. Another lefty? I must have died and gone to beautiful left-handed boy heaven (if that heaven has fluorescent lighting and smells like burnt mac and cheese).

SNACK TIME!

We get Snack Time every night before Relaxation. They bring raisins or apples or granola bars and one of those juice cups around on a cart, and we have snacks in our room. How quaint. If Sparkle is here during Snack Time, she slips me and Sandy an extra box of raisins. Tonight she told me I looked good. "You looked pretty messed up when you first got here, but now you look nice. I like your hair down."

In suckier news, I got my period tonight. I have to use hospital pads because SOMEONE forgot to pack them (OK, that someone is me, but my mom could have thought about that in my fragile state). It makes me think of when I first got my period, and my mom had to help me buy pads. We went to Cub Foods, and she let me pick out the "Teen Style" ones. Why my pads had to be stylish, I don't know. Then we celebrated with DQ. I wish she could bring me some teen pads and DQ now, because these pads suck! Not only do they not have wings, but they're so thick it's like wearing a couch in my underwear. Can you imagine how nasty it would look if I was wearing one of these with a pair of bike shorts (not that I'd even wear bike shorts)? I wonder if people can tell I have a giant pad on. It feels like I'm walking all widely, like a cowboy approaching a showdown. I hope Justin doesn't notice. Pardner.

Speaking of Justin, Sandy is in Justin's Group. I'm dying to ask her about him—what does he talk about? Who does he sit next to? Has he confessed his undying love for anyone (wink wink)? But I haven't said anything yet. I don't want her to think I'm some crushing dork. Not this soon in our friendship anyway.

Thursday, Day 7

Tracy,

Well, a week later and I still haven't actually mailed you a letter. I'm kind of afraid what they'll do at the front desk if I ask for an envelope and a stamp. Maybe they'll take my bra back or make me sleep in the hall again. I never know here.

Today I get the exciting addition of school to my schedule. I haven't been down there yet. ("School" is on a lower floor of the building. According to the elevator buttons, we live on the third floor, and there are four floors total.) Yesterday the hospital staff made me sit in my room during school hours. I did some reading from a random English textbook the staff found left over from a past inmate. I really loved the story "Kaleidoscope" by Ray Bradbury, where all of these people are floating around in space because their spaceship blew up. They still had radio contact with each other, but they knew that sooner or later they would all drift apart and lose communication. Some went crazy, others berated each other, and then in the end they all died as meteors sliced their limbs off or they burnt up in the Earth's orbit. I wonder which was the best way to die.

I have cramps. I wish I had my ugly brown cardigan here. What I wouldn't give to snuggle up in some brown acrylic. In other clothes news, my pants are definitely looser. I still don't have much of an appetite. That would be so amazing if I was actually losing weight without trying.

They're coming to get me to go to school now. More later . . .

AFTER SCHOOL

Whoa! I don't know where to start! School is cool! (Don't be a fool!) It's like this little maze of classrooms, so we get left alone a lot when one of the "teachers" (I don't think they're actual teachers, since they don't actually teach us anything. And we get to call them by their first names) has to go help someone else. I was in the same room as Matt O. and Colby, and across the hall I could see Justin, Tanya, and this short buff guy named Luther from Group A. My teachers at real school finally sent my homework, and—oh joy!—I get to read *The Crucible.* How sad that someone could write a play about witchcraft and make it so boring. Being in a school set me on edge again. The classrooms weren't full, but they were quiet. I started bouncing my knee up and down, which is what I do when the stomachaches start. I was about to ask the teacher if I could go to the bathroom when she stepped out of the room. The instant she walked away, Tanya and Luther started making out! It was totally weird and kind of gross, but also funny. I never would have thought of the two of them together, but I guess it's pretty slim pickings here. The whole time Phil/Shaggy was simultaneously peering into the hallway to see if the teacher was coming back and leering at the young lovers. I couldn't take my eyes off of Justin, who looked so cool and studious sitting next to them and writing in his notebook. Then he looked up at me, and I totally wanted to turn away but couldn't because he looked so good. Then he smiled at me, and I nearly let out a moan. Phil broke the moment by zooming back to his desk. Tanya and Luther wiped their forearms over their mouths and went back to their homework. When the teacher got back, it was as if nothing happened.

So love is possible at the Loony Bin. Or, at least, lust.

STILL IN SCHOOL

Wow. The minutes pass like hours here, just like in real school! As part of my assignment for *The Crucible*, I'm supposed to write a list of characters. However, since I can't seem to get past page three, I've decided to create my own cast of Lake Shit characters. I shall call it:

Anna's Handy Dandy Guide to All Folks of Lake Shit

Anna: Your lovable narrator, dealing with panic attacks, irritable bowels (ugh! That word!), and fatness.

Sandy: My trusty roommate, slightly white trash, who ran away from home and landed here. Has buff boyfriend back home.

Troy: Jack-assian, yet kind of hot, white guy who twists his hair into dreadlocks and gives me nasty looks.

Victor: A nice and funny guy in my Group who sold drugs at school and whose mom has cancer. At least I think she does. I don't always know what to believe here. Likes to stand near me in the elevator.

Phil/Shaggy: Sleazy guy who liked to set things on fire and who seems like a total perv.

Colby: Awkward kid who hears voices and is afraid of everything. Not very fun to hang around.

Matt O.: Nice guy in my Group who enjoyed eating dinner with me. Once had a pencil that was lost by Justin.

Tanya: Mean girl who hates me. Hates everyone, really, except Luther.

Jolene: Tanya's bowl-haired ex-roommate. She went home the week I got here.

Bobby: Younger guy who reminds me of Mara. Hit his brother (on purpose?). Seems OK.

Sean: Rosary-carrying rebel who busted out of boarding school. Scum-stache.

Justin: The beauteous yet mysterious lefty who once liked The Ramones.

Do you think it's worth an A?

NIGHT

Tonight Sandy and I went to Free Time together. One half hour after dinner, everyone who was a good boy or girl that day gets to sit around in the Day Room and hang out. Slightly fun, in a hanging-out-in-someone's-basement kind of way. This is where the real power of the Level II comes into play, because Level IIs get to decide whether we watch TV or listen to the radio and what we watch or listen to. Sean chose TV, which would have been fine with me, except that he turned on a dork-o rerun of *Full House.* Maybe the powers that be censor our television (or maybe *Full House* is the type of program that a teenager with multiple rosaries watches).

Justin sat by himself on a green fart chair in a corner, hair dangling forward as he wrote into a composition notebook. Interestingly, he wrote with his *right* hand. Ambidextrous? Be still my heart.

Since it was Sandy's first time around most of these people, I stuck close by. Plus I felt the need to block her from the grossness of Phil/Shaggy, who was stalking her, hyenalike, bragging about how he did a bunch of arson but never got caught. I wonder if Phil sets fire to things because that's the only way someone would refer to him as "hot." Ooh—I *burnt* him!

Sandy and I sat down at a table to watch Victor and Luther play a card game called Hearts. Phil went on. "You shoulda seen this one fire I started, man, everyone was yelling, 'Call 911!' and I was standing there, watching the blaze go higher and higher."

"Yeah," Victor interjected, "the blaze from a garbage can. You never started no real fires. Go away, I'm about to win this game."

Luther slammed his cards down on the table. "Shoot. Again?"

"Always," said Victor.

Walking around, listening, talking to people, I felt really . . . comfortable? The TV provided noise, so I didn't think about my stomach. Creepy Phil gave us someone to laugh at. Victor invited me and Sandy into the card game. Who would've thought I would be playing cards with a drug dealer? This place seemed to erase all social stereotypes. There was absolutely no pressure to be cool or skinny or entertaining. I was there, and that was enough.

Trying to fall asleep afterward, all I could think was that this is the first time in a long time where I feel comfortable somewhere. It's pretty fucked up that that somewhere is a mental hospital.

Friday, Day 8

Today is my one-week anniversary. I wonder what the gift is for a one-week anniversary, you know, like they show on the back of those free Hallmark calendars? Diamond for 50th, paper for 12th, or whatever. I bet it's something like a single raisin. Or perhaps a prune.

Doc Ass and I had a therapy session this morning, so I missed Group. Usually, I feel inclined to answer all questions and tell people what they want to hear, but I always feel like Dr. A. is provoking me. "I see you fixed your hair." "Are you taking your meds or just hiding them under your tongue?" "I hear you've been hanging out with the boys at lunchtime."

That set me off. "Of course I sit with the boys at lunch. There's only one other girl here. Am I supposed to sit alone?" He smiled a little, as if he liked seeing me get mad. I hate having to talk to him. I'd rather be in Group, as lame as it is. Matt O. usually whispers sarcastic comments to me under his breath. Victor always sits next to me, which makes me feel kind of good. Even Phil/Shaggy's pervy arson talk would be better than sitting with this cartoon of a psychiatrist trying to bullshit "feelings" out of me. Why should I tell him anything anyway? It was a therapist who told my parents to put me here in the first place, and she was way more screwed up than I am with her sex "theories."

At that moment I almost wanted to go home.

"When do I get to talk to my parents?" I glared at him.

"Later this week." He said he didn't have any more details, and the rest of the session was spent in silence. I'm sure he wanted me to grandly emote, but if he was waiting for me to have a revelation, that wasn't going to happen today. What does he care? Don't shrinks get paid a shitload of money whether I talk or not?

I have yet to get any mail or phone calls, and I'm curious to know what's going on in the outside world. Before Sparkle gets off her shift in the morning, she slides the newspaper under my door. It's always a day behind, but I only really read the comics and entertainment sections. Anything's better than gagging on *The Crucible*. I found an article about dance movies, so I ripped out some pictures from *Saturday Night Fever* and *Dirty Dancing* to stick on my walls. They look a bit jagged, since we can't even have safety scissors, but they brighten up the room a bit. Every room needs a little Patrick Swayze.

LATER MORNING

New girl on the floor! I don't know when she came in—this morning or last night. I discovered her when Sandy and I accidentally had our bathroom door open at the same time that Tanya's was, which is a total no-no because it could be construed as attempted socializing. We could see straight into her room, and there was the new girl lying in bed. It was no ordinary bed, even though she looked like an ordinary girl. It was a toddler's bed, the kind with metal guards on each side so no one falls out. A man wearing a sweater with a tie underneath stood by her bed and took notes on a clipboard. Sandy and I stared until the man caught us and shut the door.

LUNCH

Lunch was a big, giant butt today. Justin wasn't there because he had an appointment with his doctor, so I was stuck sitting next to Phil/Shaggy, who alternately discussed the sexy possibilities of the new girl and tried to grope my leg under the table. I was afraid I was going to get in trouble for the contact I made whilst kicking his shin with my heel.

I ate a bowl of Cap'n Crunch in memoriam of happier meals with Justin.

STUDY TIME

I was starting to feel a little claustrophobic in my room, so I stuck my two fingers out into the hallway to ask someone to open my windows. I had to wait the seven or eight minutes it took some oblivious desk worker to notice me, but finally someone came, unlocked the screens, and pushed open my windows. Aaaah—fresh air. Fresh, stanky, city air, but real air at least, not the recycled airplane air they have pumping through this place. Maybe if I sniff hard enough I can smell the cars of the future.

EVENING FREE TIME

La-dee-doo! Justin and I hung out the entire Free Time! Here's how it happened: I was sitting by a speaker because someone finally decided to turn off the *Full House* reruns and put on the radio. I was starved for music. I didn't care what station; I didn't care if it was Celine Dion belting out that sappy *Titanic* song. I just needed to hear music. There's a terrible quiet here. Farting chairs, air conditioner hums, and the incessant talking we have to do are making me antsy, but the music covered up all of the little, itchy everyday sounds. (That's why I always like going to musicals better than plays because plays are so freakin' quiet. I spend the whole time worrying about coughing or scraping my shoe on the floor in an implicating way. At musicals and concerts, the music fills up every extra bit of sound so that I don't have to worry about the sound around me.) It felt so good to have the radio on, like I could let out a giant sigh and hum all I wanted and no one would know but me. I must have looked pretty content because that's when Justin, adorable with his hands in his pockets, came and sat down next to me.

We had on a classic rock station, and Led Zeppelin was on (chosen by Level II Sean. I had no idea he listened to classic rock. I would have pegged him for a Yanni fan. Perhaps he likes the whole Zeppelin *Houses of the Holy* thing to go with his many rosaries . . .). "You like Zeppelin?" Justin asked. "They're OK," I said, because you know I'm not huge into classic rock. "I like Bonham's hard drumming," I said. Oh my god—did that sound pervy? Justin looked at me and nodded like he knew what I meant, but he didn't say anything else. "You?" I asked. "They're OK," he said. "I don't really listen to any music anymore except The Doors." "The Doors?" I asked. "Yeah. The Doors."

Let us take a moment to analyze this, shall we? My one major association with The Doors is when my cousin, Daniel, took my sister and me to a Doors laser light show in Portland, Oregon. I can't hear "Break on Through" without busting into laughter at the thought of the crazy dancing elf on the ceiling. "I guess they're kind of interesting," I shrugged. "No bass, right?"

"You know about that?" Justin seemed impressed.

"Sure. I'm kind of teaching myself to play the bass. It's hard when you like punk and the bass lines are so fast, so I pay attention to other music, too. I'm not very good, but I only do it in my basement anyway. My sister usually joins me on air guitar." Justin smiled. "How about you? Do you play any instruments?"

"Not anymore." He looked up and ruffled his hair.

"How come?" I asked.

"Long story." I waited for him to say more, but I didn't want to push. We were in a mental hospital, after all.

The rest of Free Time we just sat and listened to music. I wished Justin and I hadn't stopped talking, but sharing the music was still doing something together. It kind of felt like we were in a rec room circa 1969. Big ugly chairs, groovy music, bad lighting. No black light, thank god, because that always ends up showing dandruff or makes your teeth look freakish and glowy. I'm going to go as far as saying this was our first date. Which would make it my first date ever. I'm probably the only person on Earth who had to be committed to a mental hospital to find a date.

Saturday, Day 9
LÉ BREAKFAST

I learned more about the new girl. Luther claims he heard from Tanya (who, of course, still can't eat with us because she's a wayward be-otch) that the new girl, Abby, has seizures, and the metal guards are to prevent her from falling out of bed. Is that what they do for people with seizures? It would seem to me that hitting your head on a metal bar would be worse than hitting your head on the floor, but what do I know.

I assumed she has epilepsy, but Luther said, "No, it's something else. It's not medical. She has seizures because she's possessed by Satan." Bum-bum-bummmmm!!!

At that moment I wanted to laugh, of course, because there was now an actual measurable percentage of people here having some kind of relationship with the Lord of Darkness, but no one else was laughing. How can they take that seriously? Maybe it's just because I'm a Jew that I don't get the whole Satan possession thing, but it seems to me that these kids are just begging for attention from someone in the mental health field. Seizures and Satan possession? That's straight out of *The Exorcist*! I'll bet Abby's in my therapy group. I can just picture it: Someone will be in the middle of some huge emotional breakthrough, and all of a sudden Abby starts puking up pea soup and jabbing herself with a crucifix (or perhaps one of Sean's rosaries). I wonder if she'll get a lot of points for that. . . .

I watched Justin as the table talked about Abby. His brow was furrowed most of the time, but I did notice him roll his eyes when Luther said she was possessed by Satan. He is so cool. He's not going to fall for any of those kids' satanic shenanigans. I don't know if he's going to fall for me either (in the romantic way of falling, not that he won't believe in my existence. I hope.). I also noticed that he was eating with his left hand. He kept his right hand in his lap, under the table. Curious.

POST-COMMUNITY (NOT TO BE CONFUSED WITH POST—SHREDDED WHEAT)

I have good news and very bad news, and I don't know which to tell you first. Just so you don't worry, the bad news isn't about me. I'll tell you the good news first, but please read it in a somber tone.

At Community this morning I was totally trying to get up the nerve to stand up during Appreciation and say something about my big date (shut up) with Justin. When Eugene called "Appreciation," I was about to unfart myself from the chair when Justin outfarted me. Of course, then it seemed too stupid for me to stand up and appreciate someone who was standing up, so I just stayed down. There was the usual bland round of Appreciations: "I appreciated the way you shook the ketchup." "I appreciated you leaving the bathroom light on for me." "I appreciate that you stopped using my deodorant." When it was finally Justin's turn, he looked straight at me with his luscious brown eyes and said, "Anna, I really appreciated talking about music with you last night." If my butt was burning up as much as my face was at that moment, I would have burnt a hole into my vinyl chair.

Now for the bad news: Sandy wasn't in Community today because her doctor (who we have nicknamed Birdcage because he looks like one of those giant Muppet birds) had to meet with her. "What did he want to talk to you about?" I asked.

"It's actually something I had to talk to him about. Um . . . I'm pregnant."

At first I wondered, "Who was she having sex with at Lake Shit?" because she's only been here a few days. But then it dawned on me that the impregnation actually occurred before she came to the hospital.

She was sitting on her bed crying when I opened our door, and I wanted to hug her so badly, but I hesitated because of the no-touching rule. I can't believe that in the private space of our own room at such an important moment, I actually thought of that stupid rule. I'm brainwashed, I tell you. Then I said, "Screw it," and sat down next to her with hugs.

"What are you going to do?" I asked her.

Wiping her eyes, Sandy said, "Derek [her guy] and I talked about this before. Lots of girls at our school have babies. There's even a day care. We said if it ever happened that we'd have the baby."

"Really? A baby?" I couldn't imagine having sex, let alone having a baby. "Having a baby is a big responsibility. Not to mention how horrific birth sounds. Haven't you seen that god-awful movie in sex ed? Don't tell me that's a miracle. You sure you want to go through with that?"

"I guess. I mean, yeah. I'm already seventeen. Derek and I were gonna get married next year anyway. This way, there's no way my parents could say no to us moving in together."

Sandy looked out through the window screen pensively, her hand on her tummy. What a different life from mine. A boyfriend. Sex. Marriage. A baby? What about college? Does she know what she wants to do with her life? Or is this it? I didn't ask her because I didn't want to sound like an elitist snob. I know college isn't for everyone, but is Sandy doomed to live a trailer park existence because she made a mistake?

"What about an abortion?" I braced myself for her response. My cousin had an abortion, and so did that girl we know at school. Abortion seemed a more realistic option in my world (meaning my suburban existence, not my own personal world—unless we're talking an immaculate conception in my future), but a lot of people really are against it. I was afraid Sandy would be pissed.

"No," she answered. "I don't believe in abortion. I mean, it's OK if someone else has one, but I wouldn't feel right."

"What did Birdcage say?"

Sandy started crying again with her face in her hands. "He said I should think about abortion and realize that having a kid isn't all fun and games."

"It isn't. They made us carry around an egg in sociology class for a week and pretend it was a baby. We had to take it with us everywhere, and if we broke it we got an F. I had to get a babysitter just to go to gym class." I smiled at the memory of Eggbert.

"That's just an egg." Sandy wiped her hand in front of her face dismissively. "A real baby will be different. Think of how cute it will be. I've heard that the bond between a mother and a baby is stronger than anything else on Earth. Unconditional love." She looked dreamily at the pictures of Derek.

"Yeah. I've heard that." I don't think any of us at Lake Shit are feeling the unconditional love these days.

Sunday, Day 10

MORNING

Sandy had a private meeting with Birdcage about her pregnancy decision. When she told him that she was going to keep the baby, he freaked and said she was making a huge mistake.

After Breakfast Elevator Report: Victor continues to monopolize the space next to me. I am beginning to lose all hope that I will ever touch Justin's arm.

AFTER GROUP

I totally called it—Abby's in my Group. She is royally bizarre. She sat opposite me in our Group circle wearing hospital PJs (so she must be on PSI I, unless she just likes wearing flimsy blue clothing with drawstrings). She has a short brown feather cut and looks to be about thirteen, although I think she may be one of those older people who looks younger, due to the fact that she kept referring to her "boyfriend." I don't get it. How can some head case that sleeps in a toddler bed have a boyfriend and I don't? Am I that date–mentally challenged?

Her story belongs on *Ripley's Believe It or Not*. She filled up our whole Group meeting with her blathering on about why she was in the hospital and why she had seizures. It was rather mesmerizing. If we had to vote at the end as to whether we believed her story or not, I don't think any of us would have a clue how to answer. Judge for yourself:

"So, yeah, my name is Abby, and, as you probably know, I have seizures sometimes." She began her story in her thick Chicago accent. "The seizures just recently started to happen, though. The doctors say it's not epilepsy, or anything they can give me medicine for, ya know?" She ended most of her sentences with question marks.

Eugene was leading Group today, and in his gurgly voice, he prodded Abby to continue. "And why do *you* think you have these seizures, Abby?" He asked the question as though he was bored and didn't believe or care about anything she was saying.

"Well, my boyfriend, Angel, he's, like, really smart and really into Stephen King. When we first met, I had never even seen a Stephen King movie, 'cause, you know, I get scared when it's dark and I see scary things on the TV, but he said if I was gonna be his girlfriend I sure better start watching 'em." Abby was full of nervous energy and bounced her knees incessantly. "So every night, this was like two months ago, we watched a different Stephen King movie? We could afford it 'cause Angel's stepmom works at the video store by us. We saw *The Shining*, *It*, *Christine*. His favorite is *Carrie* 'cause he thinks she's hot, but I don't know why 'cause she's all skinny and then gets that pig's blood dumped all over her?" She quickly and dramatically reenacted the scene in her chair, first with the bucket being dumped on her head, then with Carrie's eyes bugging and accusingly looking around the room. It was quite realistic.

"Angel starts saying how it would be cool if I had telekinetic powers, so I could, like, shut doors with my brain and shit? For my birthday he bought me this book on controlling minds and he made me practice, like, every day after school and then, like, every night watch *Carrie*?"

Eugene interrupted, "And where were your parents during all of this?"

"My parents are divorced, and my dad moved up to Sheboygan, Wisconsin? My ma works second shift, so she doesn't get home until midnight. She's never even met Angel."

Eugene sighed and rolled his eyes in a "Well, there you go" way. "So, you're practicing closing doors and watching *Christine* a lot—"

"*Carrie*, not *Christine*. *Christine* is about a car? Anyways, I start getting these terrible headaches from scrunching my mind up so

I can concentrate." She squinted hard to demonstrate. "Angel said closing doors was too big to start, so then I tried pencils 'cause I thought they'd be easier? But my headaches just got worse and worse. One day, I was staring at this pencil that Angel gave me for Valentine's Day that had all these hearts on it." She held out a fake pencil and stared. "It was, like, forty-five minutes, when something in my head just popped, and the next thing I know I'm in some really foggy place. I'm calling out Angel's name, and he ain't answering. Then finally I snapped out of it, and I was in a hospital bed. My ma was there, and she told me I had a seizure. Like I said, they couldn't find anything wrong with me, so I went home. Angel and me kept working on my telekinesis. But he told me something that happened, and he told me not to tell anyone?"

Long pause. "Would you like to tell us?" Eugene asked.

"I was afraid of pissing Angel off, but it started to scare me. I mean, I didn't want to turn into Carrie, standing at the prom dripping with pig's blood? See, Angel told me that when I was having the seizure, I started talking. Only—it wasn't me. It was a deep, mean man voice that kept saying, 'I have Abby. You will not get her back.' Angel thinks it's the devil and that through my strong telekinetic powers I have brought him to me." She nodded her head at the circle of listeners.

"Would anyone like to comment on Abby's story?" Eugene looked around the circle.

Most of us looked at our feet. What was there to say? It's not like you can really give someone advice about these matters.

Then Tanya piped in, "As long as y'all don't have a seizure when I'm trying to sleep, you can do whatever you want." Always a charmer, that Tanya.

I was pretty much in shock about the whole thing. How was being in a mental hospital going to get the devil out of this girl? If he's even in there in the first place. What if she uses her telekinetic powers to lock my side of the bathroom door so I can't use the toilet? Are we going to have to get a priest in here and have some exorcism action? Is any of this for real? Believe it or not!

LATER

Tracy, I thought Sunday was supposed to be the day of rest, but not in this hellhole . . .

We had Study Time this afternoon, which is basically where I lie on my bed with *The Crucible* on my chest and fall asleep until someone comes into our room to check on us and I pretend to be reading. Sandy sat at her desk the whole time and wrote down different variations of her future married name:

Sandy Peterson
Mrs. Derek Peterson
Ms. Sandy Shelty-Peterson

I sat up and looked alert when Bettina barged into the room carrying a black babydoll with fake ball earrings punched into the side of its head. "This is your baby, Sandy. Your doctor says you have to carry it around, and feed it and burp it and change it. It's gonna teach you just what it's like to have a real baby." Cradling the doll, Bettina walked over to Sandy and placed the doll into her arms. "Be sure you support her head, now." Bettina looked at me. "Now don't give her too much help. She needs to learn to do this on her own." Bettina walked out.

Sandy and I looked at each other with furrowed brow (brows?). How is this going to teach her what it's like to have a real baby? I know they make those Baby Poops-a-Lot dolls, or whatever, that you have to stick a key into to stop it from crying (just like a real baby!), but this is just like any other doll. Not to mention Sandy and her boyfriend are as white as powdered sugar, and unless she's been having sex with a plastic black man, I cannot imagine this to be her baby.

"Let's name her," Sandy said. "How about 'Mary Jane'?"

"That's too Spider-Man. And those Mary Something names always confuse me. Is it a first name? Is it a middle name?" I thought for a second. "What about Buffy? Then she can kick ass."

"She doesn't look like a Buffy." She didn't look like a baby either, but we were still trying to name her. Then I thought of Morgan, that cute little girl you and I took trick-or-treating last year. Remember, Trace?

"Morgan," Sandy said. "I like it." She looked at the doll closely, seeing if the name matched. I told her the story of Morgan, how her mom was a black lawyer and her dad was a white doctor. They moved across the street from my house last summer. The first black person on our block. Not that it's an anti-black block; it's just more of a Jewish neighborhood. We decided to have our first neighborhood block party to welcome them. The Sutcliff family that lived next door to them—an extra-blond, non-Jewish family who you never met—refused to come to the party. We knew that they were kind of white-trashy because they always had an extra car or two junking out on the driveway. But this was how we learned they were also racist. Even though the real Morgan was just a little kid, it made her seem stronger, knowing that she already had enemies to face. I thought it was a fitting name for that plastic baby.

"Can I hold Morgan?" Sandy tossed her to me like a football. I was glad to see that she wasn't taking the babydoll too seriously, although I hoped she knew that throwing a real baby could get her imprisoned. I looked at the doll closely. It had plastic hair molded to the head, like on a Ken doll, with fake curls lining the forehead. All it was wearing was a babydoll tee (Ha! 'Cause it's a babydoll! In a T-shirt!) and a tiny, real diaper. Is that how small babies are? It must be scary to be responsible for such a mini, fragile person. Sandy seems so carefree about the whole thing. If I were pregnant, I would be shitting bricks having a living thing rolling around inside of me. I know Sandy won't consider it, but I think I would go the abortion route. There's no way I'm ready for a baby, and there's double no way I could handle going through all of the medical trauma just to put it up for adoption. I'm making myself sick thinking about this. I'm so glad it's not happening to me. I just hope that it happens to me someday. Sex, I mean. And it's not so consequential when it does. I'd settle for a first kiss at this point. . . .

POST-DINNER

Those ass-eyes won't even let Sandy come down to dinner. They say it's not safe for her new baby to be around so many germs, so Sandy's stuck in the room and I'm left alone for another exciting dining adventure.

I noticed on the elevator that Justin was several people closer to me than normal. Of course, Victor took the coveted spot next to me (Me! I'm coveted!), but I'm hoping Justin will bully his way over with his imposing height. I can't tell, because no one has ever been remotely attracted to me, but I think Justin might like me. Whenever he says something, he looks at me first to get a reaction. But maybe that's because I'm always staring at him, and they say that if you are staring at someone that they automatically have to look at you by some freaky cosmic force. Like yawning because somebody else yawns. But what if he was genuinely looking at me? I think he might have been.

Our dinner conversation was pretty interesting. Without me saying anything, everybody already knew that Sandy had to carry around a doll baby. The Rosary Boys (i.e., Colby and Sean) were all, "Abortion is wrong. The Lord would be angry." He'd probably be angry about that nasty scum-stache, too, but I'm not preaching. I was afraid Sean was about to pull out another rosary for me, but then Justin started talking about how it should be a woman's choice whether or not she wants to have a baby. Not to be all '50s gaga, but he's so dreamy! I loooooove a feminist man.

Of course, all Phil/Shaggy could focus on was the sexual act that led to the pregnancy. "Damn, I envy that guy. Do you think they were naked?"

Matt O. put another spin on things. "I don't know why anyone would want to bring another human into this crappy world. Look at us. I've been at Lake Shit for six months. Did you know that it costs our parents over a thousand dollars a day to keep us here? And the only reason most of you leave before I do is that your insurance runs out. I get to stay here because my dad thought it would make sense to buy the super-sized insurance policy. My dad would rather spend," he paused to calculate, "$180,000 than look at my sorry ass. I don't know if I'm pro-choice, but I'm sure as hell anti-child."

Six months for $180,000! I cannot believe that. For what? Crappy food and out-of-date movies?

"My parents said I'd be out of here in a week if I got better," Bobby said. "This is my third week, and nobody's told me anything. At least they finally stopped changing my meds."

"Yeah, it's nice to see you actually sitting still," Matt O. told Bobby.

"I'm out of here the second my insurance runs out," Justin told us. "My mom called last night and told me I sounded good, like it's because of Lake Shit, so they want me to stay as long as possible. I asked them how much longer I'll be here, and all she could say was, 'Not much. Your father hasn't really given me all of the details,' " he spoke in a singsong mom voice. "I don't want to see them either, then," he mumbled under his breath while stacking up his Tater Tots with his left hand.

"How about you, Anna?" Matt O. asked.

"I have no idea. I don't even know if I have insurance. My parents take care of all that, and I never paid attention. My dad's a high school teacher. Do they get good insurance?"

"The best," Matt O. answered. "You're gonna be a lifer, like me," he smiled.

I didn't want to be a lifer. Six months. I don't want to live in a sticky-walled room with thick window screens and no-lock bathroom doors for six months. I don't want to have to put my fingers out every time I want to talk for six months. I don't want to ride up and down in a no-touch elevator for six months. What if everyone at home forgets about me? What will life be like when I get out? What will *I* be like?

POST-FREE TIME

I had a very interesting chat with Matt O. tonight while we played a game of War. Justin was writing intently in a distant corner (with his right hand) in his notebook, and I didn't want to bother him.

Alone with Matt O., it seemed like an OK time to ask, "So, Matt, why are you here? You never told us in Group."

"Yeah, well, it's kind of embarrassing."

"You're not hearing voices or running with the devil, are you? How bad could it be?"

We played War as he spoke. "My parents got divorced when I was little. My dad was real good about visiting and sending money and stuff—still is. My mom worked a lot and met this guy, Ray. He moved in with us a couple of years ago." Long pause. The game continued. "He was always home because he was on disability for some factory accident with his foot. It wasn't too bad having him around for a while because he made dinner every night." Matt O. paused, and as he bit his lip I could tell something big was coming.

"You don't have to continue if you don't want," I told him. My stomach flipped as I assumed the worst. Did I want to hear this?

"They say it's not my fault, so I shouldn't feel embarrassed talking about it. It's kind of hard not to be embarrassed about some guy touching my dick." He didn't look at me, but he didn't cry either. I bet I would cry if I had to say something like that.

"Ugh," I replied. I felt gross. I don't know if it was because a grown man had touched Matt, or if just thinking about the unknown world of penises made me nervously sick. I really couldn't believe some sick fuck could do that to Matt.

"Yeah. That's a good way to put it. My dad exploded when he came by one night to visit and caught Ray in the act. Beat the crap out of him. My dad pays for me to be here so they can 'fix me,' " he said with finger quotes. "It's still stuck in my head, though."

"Is that why you're still here after six months?" Is that what they do to kids who are sexually abused? Send them away?

"Not really. I mean, I'm a lot better. Of course it's going to be in my head in some way. I kind of *choose* to stay here."

I was shocked, but at the same time I could understand it in terms of my own feelings. How easy and comfortable it is here.

"Not that Lake Shit is so great, but my dad acted so weird to me after the whole thing. We used to be so close, and now he won't even look at me. I think he's embarrassed for me or something. And my mom will hardly admit that Ray did it." Matt did an impressive one-handed shuffle and kept his eyes on the cards.

"You're kidding."

"No. My doctor tells me that's common. I guess my mom doesn't want to admit that she'd date such a dickhead. I don't want to go home and live with her again, and my dad has good insurance. So I'm here."

He looked up at me and gave a shrug.

"At least you can talk about it here, right?"

"Actually, I haven't really told many people. I must like you." He smiled.

"I guess you're kind of glad that no one's allowed to touch you while you're here?" Matt resumed our game of War. I flipped over an ace and took one of his kings.

"I wouldn't mind it so much if it wasn't some perv doing the touching. I liked it a lot when my girlfriend was doing it, you know what I mean?"

"Not so much," I said.

"What do you mean?" he asked. "Like *you* never had a boyfriend?"

"Nope," I said. "War. One, two, three, turn over." I got an ace in that War. "Sweet!"

"That's hard to believe," Matt O. said, " 'cause you're so pretty." He straightened out his dwindling deck.

"Thanks, but I think you're the first person to think that." I was beating the crap out of him in the game. All he had left was a bunch of low-numbered cards and one ace. I hoped we would have an aces War.

"Doubtful," he said, as I collected card after card of his twos and threes.

"I mean, I never thought I was ugly, but I'm, you know, kind of a pudge. Guys aren't into that, except for those weird guys who are *only* into that and go on *The Tyra Banks Show* saying how much they 'looooove them love handles.' " I guess I was trying to change the subject because I was embarrassed. No one's ever said nice things like that about me before.

"Ace War!"

"You're not fat. You're . . ." Matt O. laid out his ace and three other cards. I knew I'd win this, since the ace was his only good card and that was already showing. ". . . Juicy," he said. "Turn over."

We flipped over the cards. Mine was a king. His was a three. "You win," he smiled. "Good game."

"Free Time is over. Back to your rooms," Bettina called.

I was stunned. "Juicy." Like J. Lo or Beyoncé or, I don't know, who else is juicy? Britney Spears before the babies? Most famous people I can think of are just rods with big boobs. I mean, when I think of juicy, I think of sexy. Me, sexy? Maybe it's just because Matt O. has been here six months and is slightly delusional. And he is a teenage boy, and the only other girls here are taken, possessed, or pregnant. But he didn't have to say "juicy." He could have just gone through the usual "You're not fat" routine that my friends always give me (no offense, Tracy). I think I can live with juicy.

BEDTIME

Morgan is quite an entertaining plastic baby. She loves to play all sorts of games. Following is a short list:

① Morgan Overboard: This game involves Sandy and me standing on our respective beds and tossing Morgan back and forth as fast as we can. If we drop her, she falls into the ocean and is eaten by sharks.

② Hide-and-Seek: This is where one of us hides Morgan, and the other has to find her. I wonder what the staff here would say if they knew we were stuffing the "baby" under our mattresses.

③ Smush in Morgan's plastic face: Self-explanatory.

We get so bored in our room. Sometimes we just stare through the "protective" mesh screen over our windows and devise escape plans. The pink and blue cars are still sitting in the parking lot. Sandy has dubbed them our getaway cars, and whenever we bust out of this joint we will escape in all their pastel glory.

monday, Day 11

MORNING

TMI, I'm sure, but I'm starting to get rather hairy (only on my legs and armpits, of course. It's not like I'm growing a beard). We are not allowed razors (for the obvious reasons). It's kind of weird, but I don't really think my legs look bad with hair on them. I think it's a myth that the hair comes back thick and prickly once you start shaving—my hair is soft and supple (Eeew! "Supple" is such a gross word, but I felt compelled to use it). My armpit hair is another story. Not that it's all hard and crunchy, but I don't like it quite as much. I think it makes me sweat more. And if I'm not actually sweating more, what I am sweating is just sitting in the small tufts of hair and is making me feel all moist and gross. I want to blot my armpit with tissues all of the time. If I ever get to talk to my parents, the first thing I'm going to ask them is to send me an electric razor. We're allowed to use those, with proper supervision. Hopefully I'll get one soon. In the meantime, send dry thoughts my way.

I'm supposed to meet with Doc A-Hole today. I wonder if he has any news from home. Does he talk to my parents? What does he tell them? He's probably sharing with them the marvels of modern antidepressants. But who can even tell if the antidepressants are working when I'm in such a completely different environment than the one at home? Why can't *I* talk to my parents? What would I say to them if I did?

I have to admit (only on paper—we wouldn't want to give the adults any ideas that they're doing something right) that things aren't nearly as bad as they were when I got here. I haven't cried or had a panic attack in days. I actually go to school (albeit fake school where I don't do any work). I have friends, and, dare I say, I have a love interest? I've lost a bunch of weight. It's like the total opposite of my real life. I know Lake Shit is a long way off from a fairy tale, but there's just a teeny-weeny parallel to Cinderella. The teeniest of weenies.

POST-BREAKFAST

I still haven't been eating much. Stuffing my face doesn't seem as much fun as it used to. Maybe it's because I'm so satisfied with the way my life is going right now (yeah, right), or maybe it's because I don't really have the time or the access to food. Or maybe it's because the less I eat, the less I have to use the no-lock bathroom. Whatever the reason, the last time I was weighed the scale said I'd lost almost ten pounds!

And now for the real news: It could possibly, maybe, be official that Justin likes me. Here is what I am attempting to decipher: We were in line for breakfast in the caf; I was behind Matt O., who was behind Justin. As the line progressed, Justin somehow ended up switching positions with Matt O. so that he was directly in front of me. At first I was just looking at the back of his, well, back, and, Trace—it was gorgeous. He's like over a foot taller than me, and all I wanted to do was nestle into the back of his soft green T-shirt. I leaned in just a little, to see if I could smell him. Since we had just showered (ooh! Not together!), he had a soapy smell, mixed with his deodorant, which I imagined to be called something like "Cool Blue." At the moment of sniffage, he turned around to talk to me (and almost caught me taking a whiff of his manly goodness). I had to clear my throat so it seemed like maybe I was just dealing with morning allergies.

"What are you gonna have for breakfast?" he asked.

"Some Cap'n Crunch. What about you?"

"Oh, I always start my day with The Cap'n. Every day since I was, like, six, I ate Cap'n Crunch. It's delicious and nutritious and gives me just the right amount of energy to get me going in the morning." He looked down and shifted his mouth to one side, as if he were embarrassed for opening up his sugary secret thoughts to me. So I said, "Cereal's cool that way. You get all those vitamins and sugar at the same time. Plus, the wholesome joy of milk." He smiled and looked into my eyes for maybe two seconds before he turned around and pulled out two boxes of Cap'n Crunch from the cafeteria buffet, one for him and one for me.

So what do you think? I mean, if someone else told me that story and said a guy was acting that way towards them, I'd be all,

"He totally likes you!" But I just can't tell because it's me. I don't want this to turn into another Erik Johnson debacle. That was hideous, remember, Trace? In 7th grade that girl Doreen told me that Erik liked me, even though I'd never even talked to him. So forever I had the biggest crush on him and thought that every time I looked at him in the halls it was so mutual, our obvious connection. And then one day you and I called him, and I made him guess who I was by my voice. He kept on guessing different popular girls' names, and I had to keep saying, "No, no, no." When I finally told him who he was talking to, he had no idea who I was! But he was still all like, "Come over." So we went over to his house, and it was so awkward. Remember how he had an open box of matzo sitting on the counter, and we were trying to figure out if he was Jewish or not because he was so blond? And then the next day in school and for the rest of forever he didn't talk to me, until it was the first day of freshman year and I finally had a class with him because he was too stupid to be in any of my classes in junior high but in high school they didn't level our English classes. One day the teacher asked Erik to take attendance. He went down the list of names, marking off people he already knew. When he got to my name, he called it out and waited because he didn't know who I was! It took me months to get over him. I think what finally did it was when I caught him staring at the clock, and when I asked him what he was doing he said he was practicing for the staring contests he had with his cat.

My point is that what if Justin is just another Erik Johnson, and

I go over to his mental hospital room where he stores his matzo, and the next day he forgets I exist? I just can't be too careful. I don't understand how some people manage to date all of the time and know they look good and show cleavage and stomach and thong like that's all perfectly normal. And even if I ever lose enough weight to *want* to show my stomach to the public, I could never feel normal anyway because *I'm in a mental hospital.*

So do you think he likes me?

AFTER INDIVIDUAL THERAPY

Oh crap. Doc A-Hole told me that my parents are scheduled to call me tonight during Snack Time.

"They are pleased to hear that you are doing so well," A-Hole said.

"You told them I was doing well? Why did you say that?"

"Well, you've moved up Levels, the teachers say you're doing fine in school, you haven't gotten any Restrictions, and according to your charts, you're losing weight."

That disgusted me. Do all of the doctors monitor all of the patients' weights, or is it just the fatasses? If some skinny guy was losing weight, they would be all over it. I lose weight, and they want to celebrate. I mean, so do I, but *they* don't need to be so happy about it. It sounds like the reason I'm doing so well is that I'm not doing anything wrong. What else is new?

I'm so nervous about talking to my parents. I wonder if it'll be both of them, or if only my mom gets on the phone. My dad's usually asleep by 8:00. I know I have to ask them for the electric razor, but then what? Why do I have to wait all day? My stomach is starting to hurt.

LATER

This place sucks. During Community, I was totally planning on standing up and saying how I appreciated Justin for, I don't know, talking and eating with me or something, and when they called "Appreciation" I even put my fingers out for the first time. Justin put his fingers out, too, but I'll never know if he was planning on commending me for my juicy body because before any of us kids were allowed to Appreciate, Eugene made an announcement. "Appreciations have been getting repetitive lately, so we've decided that there will be no more Appreciations about eating meals or chatting with people. You guys are wasting our time trying to get points just because you talked to someone. This time is for real Appreciations only."

Everyone who had their fingers out put them down, except for Matt O. When Eugene called on him, Matt O. stood up, smirked, and said, "Eugene, I appreciate what a fat bastard you are."

Everyone laughed. In the real world, I can't imagine anyone saying something like that and me thinking it sounded cool, but in here it seemed like the most excellent, rebellious thing ever. "Matt," he said. "Go to the Quiet Room." I swear I could see steam coming out of Huge Euge's ears.

"But I didn't do anything," Matt whined. His shiny eyes looked worried.

Eugene mumbled into his walkie-talkie, and soon two of the T-shirt-tucking men from the Harold incident appeared. Eugene pointed at Matt O., and the men walked towards him.

"What the fuck? I didn't do anything!" Matt jumped up and began to run, bowling over one of the two men. The other followed him out. We could hear Matt O. yelling and feet pounding, and then a door slammed. Community was completely quiet.

LUNCH

Lunch was anxiety-filled with the impending parental phone convo. Matt O. was locked in the Quiet Room, so Justin and I had our first official Anna and Justin Solo Lunch Chat. We sat at the end of the table, opposite each other. He ate with his left hand and, as usual, kept his right hand on his lap. I had to know. "Why do you eat with your left hand but write with your right?" I cringed when I realized how stalker-esque I sounded.

Choking on a chip, he asked, "You noticed that?"

"Well, yeah. I've always been interested in the right-handed, left-handed thing, and I thought it was cool that you were left-handed. Which I thought you were, since you eat with your left hand, but then I wasn't sure because I saw you writing with your right hand." Oh my god. I was so not helping my stalker case.

He smiled a little. "You're very observant."

"Yeah, well, there's not much to look at here at Lake Shit, you know?" Was I hitting on him?

"Um, thanks, I think." He looked down and slowly lifted his right hand to the table and set it down close to my tray. "This is why I eat with my left hand." It was my first good look at his right hand. His pointer and middle fingers were pudgy and misshapen. The skin was glossy, and there were several pink scar markings. "I don't want to gross anyone out while they're eating," he said, "so I keep my hand under the table."

"It's not that gross," I said, although it was a little. The shiny skin looked almost waxy. "What happened?" I asked, looking up at him.

He didn't look back at me, but brought his hand back to his lap. "I'll tell you some other time. Like I said, I don't want to gross anyone out."

I nibbled on a pretzel until he decided he wanted to talk to me again. "So how come you have so many Ramones T-shirts?" he asked.

I gushed, "They're my favorite band. They make me feel like it's possible, you know, that maybe I could be a musician someday because their songs are simple but amazing."

Justin surprised me. "I used to have this bootleg concert video, and I couldn't believe how crazy they were on stage. They look kind of old and mellow in pictures."

"You have a bootleg video of The Ramones?" I couldn't believe it. "What about the almighty Doors?"

"I *used* to have it. That was a long time ago," he said, chewing on his sandwich and swishing some OJ around in his mouth.

It's not like we're eighty years old. How long ago could he have been into The Ramones that he could switch over so dramatically to The Doors? And what happened to his hand? I wish I was some teen super-sleuth so I could solve the mystery.

STUDY TIME

Sandy and I aren't really in the mood to do homework. It's not like anyone back at school really cares if I do it anyway. Supposedly, I do my work and it'll get sent to my teachers back at real school, but nobody is giving me any actual work to do. Yeah, there's *The Crucible*, but my English teacher didn't say I have to actually do much once I read it (except gag at how lame it is). Mrs. Downy, my art teacher at school, sent me a box of colored pencils and paper, as if the plastic walls I'm surrounded by are going to inspire me to create a masterpiece. She assigned us a collage project when I was at school, where we had to create a collage from magazine clippings and then draw the collage with colored pencils. Mine's so bad. I don't know why I decided to make it based on the life and death of Aaron Spelling. At the time we got the assignment, I thought it was pretty funny and easy, since there are pictures from his TV shows everywhere.

But now that I'm stuck with these overlapping images of Heather Locklear's fried hair, I don't know how I'm going to draw all of the faces. I get stuck on the noses. Every person I've drawn so far looks like a jack-o'-lantern.

I wonder what Mrs. Downy thinks about sending colored pencils to a student in a mental hospital. She knows me relatively well, as I've taken classes with her since freshman year, but I've never really been one of those stars of art class. I guess I don't wear enough black or have enough piercings or smoke enough clove cigarettes. I'd rather hang out in the darkroom for photography anyway. At least there it's more technical, which I think I'm better at. No noses to mess up in photos. Mrs. Downy didn't include a note with the pencils. Maybe she doesn't know where I am. What if no one else does? What if something happens to you, Tracy, and something happens to my family, like all of you are abducted by the future car people, and then no one knows where I am! Lucky for me, the future cars haven't moved yet.

LATER

Matt O. is still in the Quiet Room. It's not all that quiet, though, because the room is right next to me and he keeps pounding on the wall and yelling, "Hey, Anna! Hey, Sandy! Wut up?" Then he goes through his "proclamation" over and over again. "When I die, I want them to bury me facedown and ass up so that the whole world can kiss my ass!" I don't quite get what he means, but it sounds funny as shit. Where did he even get that? I don't know how funny it would be in the real world, but right now I can't stop laughing. I hope I don't get in trouble.

Sandy hasn't gotten any homework from her teachers yet, so we just spend most of our Study Time doing one of the following three things:

1. Staring out the window and planning our escape. The pastel cars are always taunting me with their futuristic, yet retro, styling. I still can't tell what the building across the street is. If it is a hotel, then it's not a very nice one judging by the rusty old vans that are always pulling up at what appears to be the check-in.
2. Talking to the "spy cameras." Sandy and I are convinced that the light fixtures in our room have cameras in them where all of the pervy workers watch us get undressed. Sometimes we do faux stripteases for them, but I feel gross and just assume no one would want to see me stripping anyway.
3. Decorating. We've got quite a little art gallery going. They won't give us any tape, and you can be damned sure we can't get any tacks, but if we stick a piece of paper against the wall and dig our nail into the corners, it usually stays pretty well. Sandy's got a lot of photos up of her boyfriend, but all I can manage in the way of dudes is ripping out movie star photos

> from the Friday section of the newspaper. I wish they'd stop putting pictures of Ben Affleck in it 'cause there's no way I'm putting his nasty ass on my wall. The best I could do was a picture of Orlando Bloom dressed as Legolas, even though he is way hotter with his normal brown hair and eyes. I also got a picture of The Donnas rocking out. I wish I had the confidence to play the bass in public and have my hair go all crazy like that.

The room still looks kind of sad, with pictures of her boyfriend she can't even see or talk to and my newspaper pictures with raggy edges because I can't use scissors to cut them out. We decided to use my colored pencils and paper to draw portraits of each other. I was pleasantly surprised at the lack of chins Sandy drew on me. When I had to do a self-portrait in art class, I looked like a droopy dog. One could even call her drawings flattering, not *fattering*. In the last hour we've managed to do ten total (I did six in a more abstract, slashy style, and she did four, neatly and precisely). I've never really done any kind of art outside of school, except for writing. Does writing count? I write all the time, but I don't know if anyone would consider it art. Tracy, maybe you can gather all of the letters I write you (when you finally get them, of course), and when I'm ninety-seven years old and withering away in a loony bin you can publish them. We'll split the profit, 50/50. Ah, you can have it all actually. I can't do anything with money here anyway.

THE PHONE CALL

Not that I know what it would be like to be escorted to my own execution, but that is how I felt when Sparkle knocked on my door and told me my parents were on the phone. She took me into the Day Room, where brown carrels acting as phone booths were set up on several tables. Sean was at one table, sitting silently but rolling his eyes at whatever the person on the other end of the phone said. Bobby hid his head deep in the carrel, and I heard him crying and saying, "C'mon, Mom, please? I thought you wanted to visit. Can't you change your schedule?"

As I approached the table, my stomach rolled around, and I thought about leaving to go to the bathroom. "You get ten minutes," Sparkle said. "Then it's Relaxation time."

I sat down, put the receiver to my ear, and said, "Hello?"

"Anna?" My dad's voice was on the other end. Then my mom's, "Anna!" They both had an extension. "Don't yell, Beth," my dad said to my mom. "It's loud when we both have a phone."

"So how are you, honey?" My mom's voice sounded sweet, like she was trying to be calm for me.

"Um, OK, I guess."

"We miss you," my mom interrupted. "And we're sorry." I heard snuffling and sniffing; someone was crying. Since my mom was talking, I realized with horror that it had to be *my dad.*

"What are you sorry for?" I asked.

"For bringing you there without more warning. For not being able to help you ourselves."

Then I was choking back tears. I didn't want to cry. I wanted them to know I was mad, that I was tougher now and I didn't need them. But everything spilled out when I said, "Why'd you do it, Ma?"

"We didn't know what to do. You were so different, so sad all the time. You wouldn't go to school and you wouldn't go out. You used to be so . . ." She paused, and I knew what was coming. ". . . Good."

How was I so bad now? All of these kids here—drugs and devils and fire—and all I did was stop going to school. "I was never bad, Mom."

"Of course not, Annie, but you were different. You changed, and we couldn't help you. You wouldn't listen to us, and we were worried about your future. We just want you to be happy. To be better." My mom's voice broke then, and I began to feel guilty. I could hear my dad breathing unevenly in the background. I almost never saw my mom cry, and I don't think I saw my dad drop a single tear in my life, and now because of me they were both crying. Good, I thought for a minute. But then I just felt bad that I had done something to make them upset.

"I'm getting better," I told them, my tears ending.

"Really, Anna? That's so good to hear," my dad finally joined in. "We just want the best for you. We can't wait until you come home. We've been working on your room, painting and redecorating. We think you'll like it."

"My room?" I didn't like the sound of that. I love my room.

Did they think changing my room would make things different when I got back? I wanted to ask, but Sparkle came at that moment to get me.

"I have to go. Say hi to Mara for me, OK?"

"We love you, Anna. We'll talk to you soon." The call ended with overlapping exclamation of loves and misses. "You, too," I said aloofly. I couldn't let them know that I wasn't all that angry with them anymore. How could I be? They sounded remorseful, and even a little pathetic. Plus, if I weren't here, I might not be losing weight, or making new friends, or falling hard for an ambidextrous Doors fan.

Shit. I forgot to ask them about the razor.

Tuesday, A Day of Death (Day 12)

Ha! Remember that story I wrote and performed for creative writing class during freshman year about Taco Tuesday in the caf? Here, I can remember it:

Tuesday: A Day of Death

By Anna Bloom

As I casually stepped into the dark, crowded lunch line, I could tell this was no ordinary lunch day. Yes—it was Taco Tuesday. The thick, burnt stench of the so-called meat lingered in the air. Putrid pieces of soggy taco shells randomly lay on the dull silver counter next to me. I ever so slowly trudged my way ahead to the stained counter and wearily said to the lady, "Uh, taco salad?" I heard a squish, like someone shoving their hand into a vat of brains. After that there were a couple of silent plops, and a thin Styrofoam tray was handed to me. I stared down at the monstrosity. Lugging the vulgar dish to my table near the window, I saw the other disgusted faces of weary students as I passed them. Placing the mass on the table, I stared at the grotesque mound of hard, muddy meat covered in a thick, nauseating chunk of pink sauce, which looked like a combination of ketchup and sour cream. I decided to declare it a National Health Hazard and took it over to the garbage can adjacent to me. Not to my surprise, the garbage can had the same staggering odor that the taco salad did. I bent over and stared. In the garbage can was a large mass of trays identical to the one in my hand. I tossed it in and went to get a candy bar.

Wasn't I a clever little freshman? So many adjectives! Now Tuesday is officially the Day of Death because (brace yourself) Satan has arrived at Lake Shit. He has come in the form of a sixteen-year-old boy named Lawrence. Six foot five, dark skin, huge shop class–looking glasses, and skinny-as-hell with enormous feet. I don't actually believe he *is* Satan, but what Lawrence believes . . . I can laugh at Colby and his D&D voices and even at Abby with her possessed seizures, but Lawrence has actually kind of freaked me out.

He was introduced at Community this morning. He sat in the chair next to me, and the entire meeting he was panting with what can only be described as evil. Eugene asked him to stand up and introduce himself. When Lawrence stood up, he looked like a tree, swaying in the breeze with each dark breath.

"I am Lawrence," he said in his Darth Vader–deep voice. "Satan is my lord."

I swear Sean gasped and grabbed for his rosary. Sandy, who had Morgan sitting on her lap, covered the doll's eyes.

Eugene didn't buy into it right away. "Why don't you tell us a little more about yourself, Lawrence?"

"I worship the Dark Lord."

"That's fine, Lawrence [it is?], but we would like to hear about something other than your beliefs."

"Beliefs?" Lawrence's breathing increased to full-on heaving. "You belittle my master. He will not be pleased." This guy seriously talked like that!

"Lawrence." Eugene stood up, about a foot and a half shorter than the evil giant, and said, "This is the last time I will ask you to tell us something *else* about yourself. If you cannot do that, I'm going to have to give you a Restriction."

"My lord will not be pleased with you and your doubters." His doubters? Don't be draggin' me into this!

Eugene sat down and flipped open his notebook, where he kept track of points and things. "Restriction." He made an exaggerated tick mark in his book.

Raging, Lawrence leaped out of his chair, and with one stroke of his extremely long arm he banked Eugene across the face. With a roar, Lawrence ran out of the Day Room.

Eugene held his mouth and choked out a few coughs. Another staff member came in and dismissed us from Community.

As we all left the Day Room, I could hear people breathing in, as if they were about to begin a sentence but had to stop themselves because we aren't allowed to talk to each other in the hall.

Justin walked up next to me, and I looked up with an apprehensive smile and mouthed, "Pretty weird, huh?" He nodded and then reassuringly pinched my pinky with his left hand.

I realize, T., that this should have been the pinnacle of my story. I mean, no guy has ever touched me on purpose like that, let alone the finest boy on the loony block, but I am so freaked out by the psychoness that is Lawrence that even Justin's lusty hand-touching comes in a distant second in today's events.

You're probably wondering why this even bothers me, I mean, seeing as how you and I used to pretend we were satanists sophomore year. (Flashback to Mr. Judson, my math teacher, making me turn my Claire's cross earrings right side up.) But us wearing black nail polish and flashing the "Satan" hand signal at each other does not a satanist make. Nor did when we used to talk about our "goat sacrifices" during basketball in gym class to see if anyone noticed. Remember? "That goat put up a pretty good fight last night, eh?" "Yeah, and I thought I'd never get all the blood out of the curtains." Why did we think that was cool again? Not that I actually believe in the satanic aspect of Lawrence's satanism, but he sure seems a lot more evil than we did. (In fact, didn't people just think we were lesbians?) Before today, I had never actually heard the sound of someone hitting someone. It was like a hollow pop, but maybe that's because there's not much in Eugene's head. Satanist or not, Lawrence seems highly capable of spastic, unpredictable, violent behavior, and that's more real to me than the devil is.

TUESDAY AFTERNOON

Woo-woo! Love is in the air (and Lawrence is in the Quiet Room chanting prayers to his big, scary man). On the elevator down to school, Justin finally stood next to me. We both stood really still, staring straight ahead. Nothing happened for the first few seconds (Minutes? Hours? It seemed like forever), but soon I felt a little tickle on the back of my right hand. At first I was going to jerk it up and scratch it, but as it became less tickly and more warm and smooth, I realized it was Justin's hand. Back to back, the hair on our hands danced and played for the rest of the elevator ride. I closed my eyes and melted into the elevator wall. Having any contact here is exciting, but this contact was exquisite. And, if I may say even though I'm no expert, highly erotic. There were definitely other parts of me heating up besides my hand.

The ka-chunk of the elevator door popped my eyes back open, and all of the other boys came into focus. I was let off of the elevator first, and Eugene stepped between me and any of the boys getting off to prevent contact. But, *oh*, we had contact.

EVE

This afternoon everyone went to "Physical Therapy." Eugene and Bettina took us up in the elevator to the top floor of the building. For a moment it felt like the elevator was taking us to heaven. As the doors opened, the light from all of the unscreened windows made the entire floor blinding white. We squinted our way to a small gym.

Physical Therapy ended up not being much like therapy at all, but more like remedial gym class. The gym was filled with workout machines from the '80s. All we did was get on a piece of equipment and pretend to exercise, and every five minutes a staff person told us to rotate. The thing was, I knew we weren't getting showers after this, so my biggest workout was trying not to break a sweat. Some of the guys were totally pumping iron ('80s term for an '80s gym). Sean took his shirt off when he got to the weight-lifting station, but Eugene made him put it back on (he was probably jealous). At least we were allowed to talk to the people at our station. Girls and girls, boys and boys only, but still. Our station had me, Sandy, and Abby. Bettina gave Sandy a cardboard box with a pillow stuffed inside to carry Morgan around. How realistic—if you live in a tree house.

Abby was less annoying than I expected. Kind of immature and white-trashy (she thinks reruns of *Married with Children* are funny), but whatever. At one point in our workout regime (I believe we were on stationary bikes) Lawrence started freaking out, lifting one of those giant barbells above his head over and over again really fast. As he did it, he was seething and frothing at the mouth (slight exaggeration), and the whole time he was staring right at Abby. Sandy and I were cracking up because it just seemed so cartoonish, but when Abby pointed out that he was staring at her and we all looked at him and he kept staring . . . Shivers.

Speaking of shivery, Justin wasn't looking so bad in his workout mode. Thank god he wasn't all gung ho ('cause you know I like my men gangly like Joey Ramone. That's "my men" in a theoretical sense), but there was something strangely appealing about watching him lift weights. Perhaps he was sending off manly sweat pheromones that I was helpless against absorbing.

I had some anxiety about the whole workout thing. Tracy, you have watched me excuse my way out of countless gym classes. Anything to avoid running. I'm afraid of someone watching my body jiggle and sweat if I'm exercising, but I'm also afraid of looking like a fat, lazy slob if I'm not. Besides needles, my biggest fear in life is the twelve-minute run. I know everyone else in gym class is concerned with their best time and their bogus fitness goals, but I can't help feeling like every time I run (i.e.: shuffle/walk), there's a giant spotlight over me so people can laugh at the pathetic sight. Luckily, the majority of us in the Lake Shit workout room were more concerned with socializing than exercising, so at least I looked normal here.

The most fun part of Physical Therapy (besides the obvious joys of exercise—*as if*) was that there was a radio playing the whole time. True, it was on a classic rock station, but I couldn't resist singing along when "Lola" by The Kinks came on. In fact, it was a regular nuthouse sing-along. I was totally surprised that almost everyone knew the words. Victor sang along, and so did Phil/Shaggy. Lawrence didn't, but that might have been expecting too much. Bobby did that thing where you sing the words directly after they are said so it sort of looks like you know what you're saying. No one stopped us as we belted out, "Lo-Lo-Lo-Lo-Lola!" Did you know that song's about a man who gets the hots for a woman who's really a man? Even though the man-woman Lola was kind of fucked up, the guy singing was just as fucked up for believing her. Everyone's fucked up in some way, and here we were together singing our own fucked-up chorus. I'll never hear that song the same way again.

SNACK-ATTACK

Tonight we had a special treat. It was Colby's fifteenth birthday, and his parents dropped off a big chocolate birthday cake with blue food–colored frosting. I wonder if they put a file in the middle of it (not that there are bars or anything to saw through, although I suppose he could work on the window screens). Not that anyone even knew it was his birthday before they brought the cake, and not like we got to sing "Happy Birthday" to him or even thank him for giving us cake, since the pieces just came around, pre-cut on a tray, to our room. Not that I'm complaining. Cake is cake. There is no other food in the world as consistently pleasing to me, besides pizza. Mmmm—pizza. The staff claims that if enough people earn enough points to move to Level III, we'll have a pizza party on a Friday night. Oh, to be a Level III. The funny thing is, I have not seen a single person on the floor make it to Level III. They probably rig the points system so that they don't have to spend the extra $9.99 on a pizza. Anyway—back to the cake story. Sparkle brought around cake and milk to our room, and Sandy scarfed her cake before Sparkle could even leave the room.

"Damn, girl, you act like you're eating for two!" Sparkle said with a wink. When Sandy told her that she actually was eating for two, Sparkle laughed really loudly and smacked the wall with the palm of her hand. When the eruption subsided, she handed Sandy a second piece of cake! I was quite excited and jealous. Sparkle must have seen the drooly look in my eyes, because she gave me a second piece, too. She was the first adult who has been nice to Sandy about being pregnant.

Did I tell you that some weirdo from the night crew comes into our room every night to tell Sandy that she needs to feed and change Morgan? I'm getting less sleep because of it. The nerve! I didn't ask to have a baby. On top of Morgan interrupting my sleep, this week a woman has been peeking into our room every single hour during the night. She carries a clipboard and appears to be checking things off, I'm guessing about our sleeping habits. The joke is that every time she opens the door it clicks and leaks in the light from the hallway, so I wake up. Last night she looked at me, awake, and alarmingly asked, "Are you having trouble sleeping?" And I said, "Yes. Some woman keeps opening the door and waking me up."

Wednesday, Day 13

We had another new arrival today—a girl. Her name is Callie, and she's all ghetto chic, yet totally white. Because she just got here, she had a butt-load of makeup on. It'll be a rude awakening tomorrow morning when she finds out that they confiscated her lip gloss.

Everyone got a good look at Callie sitting at her desk in the hallway as we went down to breakfast. There was an air of excitement in the elevator from the boys, as if they all had hard-ons that were sending off static electricity. (So gross! Sorry—it's the first image that came into my head.)

As Justin and I munched on bowls of Cap'n Crunch and debated the merits of American vs. British punk (I said most British bands were trying too hard with their image, while the Americans were often too lax about learning how to play their instruments well), the rest of the table seemed fixated on Callie. In the past whenever guys have ogled gals, I never have felt even in the same league—not even the same species. Not female. Like there was no way a guy would ever ogle me, so why even try to look good or bother dressing nicely or whatnot because there was no point to it. Instead, I always thought I could just wear baggy pants and band T-shirts because they were comfy, and at least I felt cool. But there's been this weird shift since I've been at Lake Shit. It's like I'm the last girl on Earth, and people *have* to choose me. I feel like a woman. W-O-M-A-N. The sucky thing is now that there's another female here, I mean one who isn't pregnant or possessed by Satan, and especially one who wears makeup and clothes that actually fit her, I kind of feel like my old self. Like I should go to the back of the Woman line and stop pretending that I'm something more than I am—just an anxious chubby girl with long brown hair who likes to listen to music and worships boys who will never like me back.

POST-GROUP THERAPY

Well, thank someone (I don't know who to thank these days—God? Satan? The Dungeon Master?) Callie is not in my group, so I don't have to contemplate my body-image bullshit for at least that hour. That means Group can carry on normally, if normal happens to include a satanist in love. Read the gripping account of my Group meeting today. Feel free to act it out as a Reader's Theater.

EUGENE: Lawrence, what is going on with you today?

LAWRENCE: Love.

EUGENE: Yes, Lawrence, we know you think you love Satan.

LAWRENCE: My love is beyond Satan now. I love [dun-dun-duuunn!] Abby. [Deep gasps and snickers from the audience.] The Dark Lord has told me she is to be my bride.

ABBY: Hell no! [Faux ghetto speak] I ain't ready to be no one's bride, and certainly not *your* Satan-worshipping ass.

LAWRENCE: The Dark Lord told me you would respond in this way and that it may be necessary to take more drastic measures to win your love. I will unveil my plan soon.

I swear that's how Lawrence talks! It's like he should be standing on a stage holding a skull with a spotlight on him every time he says something. I have no idea how Lawrence chose Abby to be in love with (is it weird that I feel just a little jealous that a giant satanic freak didn't choose to be in love with me?), but I have a feeling it has something to do with her brush with Satan during her seizure. Perhaps he thinks Satan will be pleased and turn him into a personal assistant.

For our second act of Group Therapy Reader's Theater, let us enjoy this tasteful discussion of teen lust I like to call "Pervs with Problems."

EUGENE: We on staff have been noticing lately that y'all are getting a little hormonal [hee-hee]. I must remind you that there are to be no relationships of the boyfriend/girlfriend variety.

ME: What if someone's gay? Is that OK then?

EUGENE: None of that either. No touching. No whispering sweet nothings in each other's ears. And definitely no making out in school. We've got our eyes on you.

TANYA: On who? [Waking up from her regular Group nap.]

EUGENE: Don't think we don't know, Tanya.

TANYA: Know what? What a wonderful student I am? [I don't see how she gets any work done with all of the lap dances she gives Luther in school.]

EUGENE: I don't want to see it, and no one here wants to see it either.

MATT O.: Amen!

PHIL/SHAGGY: Speak for yourself.

It is pretty gross being forced to watch people make out in school. It's almost like being in real school, where Julie Ganty and Chris Panlin are always groping in front of my locker. They're pretty nice about moving, but it makes me feel doggish to have to ask. *And* that no one has to ask me. However, if they've "got their eyes on us" then why haven't they ever stopped people from making out? If I were an adult, I would feel like a total perv having to walk up to some teenagers and say, "Can you please get your tongue out of her mouth and your hand off her ass and get back to work?" That's like acknowledging that you were watching and probably why schools have No PDA rules, but no one ever enforces them. The last thing I would ever want is Eugene separating me from Justin in a passionate embrace. Dare to dream.

PLAY THERAPY

I just returned from the weirdest thing. They called it "Play Therapy." Only a handful of us were there, while the rest were at something called "Tough Love." I feel so immature, like why did I have to play while other people got some tough lovin'? Actually, I could have played all day because Justin was in Play Therapy with me. Swoon.

Some flaky woman with the craziest giant black hairdo—like, so over-the-top *Hairspray the Musical* you wouldn't believe it—brought us up in the elevator to the top floor (with only five of us in the 'vator, it was hard to get any arm-touching action without being obvious). The light in the room was gray, although it was warmer than the screened-in light of our floor. The only furniture was a circle of (nonfarting) chairs. Why are they always seating us in circles? So we don't kill ourselves on the corner of a square setup? Anywho, the hair lady, who I shall now call "Big 'Do," spoke in what she thought was a soothing manner. I wondered whether it was condescending or genuine. Big 'Do explained, "Welcome to Play Therapy. For those of you new to the experience, I hope you will find this a refreshing way to look at your 'issues.' [Finger quotes here.] Play Therapy allows us to use our imaginations to free us from the constraints of physical walls. . . ." She went on from there, but that calm voice and the rocking motion of her 'do nearly put me to sleep. The gist of it was that we were given a topic, and we had to use our imagination to re-create that topic physically without actually using anything tangible, except the other people in the room. Of course, the people weren't actually tangible either, since we aren't allowed to touch anyone. Does any of this make sense? No? Example: Today the topic was "safe places." We had to sit for way too long and think about what our favorite safe place was. Then we had to use what was in the room (i.e., the chairs and the humans) to re-create that place.

Big 'Do set the rules, "You must guide each other with your voices. If you describe the scene well enough, it will fall into place organically." What does "organic" mean when it's not describing fruits and vegetables? The whole thing was a little flaky. I thought this could have been my chance to get a little arm-on-arm action with Justin, but not a chance. The 'Do watched us like a hawk with big hair. Any time one of us got close to touching an arm, she would give a "gentle cough" as a reminder of the rules.

I chose to re-create my bedroom. I set up Sandy as my stereo (with Morgan as a speaker), Victor as a Willy Wonka poster, Colby as my bulletin board with the collage of punk and skater hotties you and I made, and Justin as—you guessed it—my bed.

"Wonderful! Wonderful!" Big 'Do exclaimed. "This says a

world about you without you having to say anything at all. Now, go play!"

"Play what?" I asked her.

"Play like you are in your safe place. Use your safe objects and show us all how good it feels to be in this place."

I walked over to Sandy and pretended to push her nose in as if I were turning the stereo on. I was this close to pretending her boobs were the radio knobs, but I thought better of it. Instead, she held up her fingers like buttons, and I pretended to put a CD in.

"And what kind of relaxing music are we listening to?" Big 'Do asked.

"The Dead Kennedys," I answered, knowing this was not the answer she was looking for. Bobbing my head to the "music," I walked to the Willy Wonka poster and the bulletin board and pretended to admire them by putting my hand on my chin and stroking it. I soon realized that people only do that when they have beards, and stopped. Victor cracked a wicked grin, and I was glad to see that Big 'Do allowed it. I smiled back. I could almost hear the corners of our mouths squeaking after not having used our smile muscles for so long, like the Tin Man in *The Wizard of Oz*. "Oil. Can."

I slowly approached Justin. I made him lie down on the floor, arms to the side, legs straight out, to give the illusion of a bed. What was I supposed to do? I would've freaked if I could actually have lain down on him (although I would also have been petrified that I would crush him). I looked at Big 'Do and said, "This is my bed. I like to lie on top of my bedspread and listen to music."

"Go ahead, dear, just do it without touching." Did she expect me to levitate? I overexaggerated a fake yawn and stretched, then slowly placed myself on the floor parallel to Justin. I turned on my side and curled into a loose fetal position. I could see the side of Justin's face, the patches where he was starting to grow hair and the patches where he couldn't. He had a small layer of fuzz on the rim of his ear, which looked like it had a velvety animal quality. All I wanted to do was reach out and touch it, touch him. I could hear his breathing, and I tried to align mine with his. It was almost impossible because I was so afraid of him hearing my breathing and thinking that I had fat person breath that I kept holding my breaths, until they ended up coming out in quick puffs. Justin's chest rose slightly, and I saw the corner of his mouth spread. He was quietly laughing. I totally thought it was because of my breathing, but then he turned so his whole face looked in my direction and said in the quietest of voices, "This is pretty weird, huh?"

I let out a relieved sigh (but made sure not to do it in his direction in case my breath stank) and smiled, "Yeah."

It was weird being in my "bedroom." I haven't thought about it in a while, how much time I used to spend there. I wonder what my parents are doing to it. My posters better be in the exact same place when I get back. What if Mara has moved into my bedroom now that I'm gone? She was always complaining about how much bigger my room was. Nah, she'd never do that. She loves hanging out in her big sister's room, I can tell. My bedroom door is the only one that she knocks on before she comes in. I miss her. But right now the only bed I'd like to be in is the one in front of me.

"Do I make an OK bed?" he asked me. Before I could think of a witty yet somewhat seductive remark, Big 'Do said, "Victor, it's your turn."

Foiled by The 'Do.

You will die when you hear what Victor's safe place was: Wal-Mart. Isn't that hilarious? Everyone busted up laughing when he said that, and Big 'Do told us that everyone is entitled to their own safe place without being laughed at.

"That's alright," Victor told her, "the only reason they laughing is 'cause they know Wal-Mart is safe 'cause I never got caught shoplifting there." He thought this was very funny, and I wondered how serious he was. I remembered what he said back in Group about his mom having cancer. "I'm just playin'. It's like they got everything I need right under one roof. And have you tried the popcorn from the snack bar?" I had, actually, and he was right. Quite good.

Big 'Do interjected, "I seem to recall from your files that your mom works at Wal-Mart."

"You read my files?"

"It's part of my job to get to know all of you," 'Do explained calmly.

"Well, yeah, she used to work there. In customer service. Before she got sick." Victor looked at Big 'Do accusingly. "Thank you *so much* for bringing that to everyone's attention."

"I'm sorry. I thought that was part of your safe place exploration." 'Do looked concerned in a glazed way. The rest of us waited. I wondered if Victor would cry.

Victor glared at Big 'Do for several seconds, then dropped his head and balled his hands into fists. He took one big breath, then another. Quite suddenly, he lifted his head and announced, "Free popcorn for everyone. Anna, you stand over here." And like that he directed each of us to our places amongst Wal-Mart's rollbacks and cheap clothing. I admired Victor for being able to hold it together like that. I hoped that someday I could be that strong.

Sandy chose her grandparents' house as a safe place. I got to be her grandpa's favorite old recliner. Justin was the TV set that still had a rabbit ear antenna. All Sandy wanted to do was sit around and watch game shows.

Colby didn't have a safe place. "This is Play Therapy, dear," Big 'Do urged. "Pretend you have a safe place." This didn't help Colby, and he chose to pass.

"If I had known we could pass, maybe I woulda done that," Victor argued.

"We're very proud that you didn't, Victor." Big 'Do smiled knowingly.

"Speak for yourself," Justin said. "My popcorn was stale."

"And mine didn't have enough butter," I joined in.

Victor looked at Justin and me with a grateful smile on his face.

Justin's safe place was, as expected, very cool. He set us up as his 1989 maroon four-door Volvo that his uncle Barney, a mechanic, fixed up for him. Victor was the obnoxious horn, which he took the liberty of demonstrating every time the room seemed just a little too quiet. Sandy and Morgan were the brake lights. Colby was a bumper sticker that said "Fight Racism," and I was his stereo. Each time he pretended to turn me on (ah, who's pretending?), I blared a little piece of a Doors song. He laughed, changed the station, and I sang a different song. "When you're strange . . ." Turn turn. "Come on, baby, light my fire . . ." Turn turn. "Love me two times, baby . . ." He kept me on this channel, and I struggled to remember the words. I tried to use my best, sexy singing voice. As Justin sat in a chair in front of me and I stood, his radio, I felt so in control. My voice has never been a thing I hated about myself, and I could tell Justin wasn't hating it at all. He even joined in and sang with me! I stopped singing for a second to hear his voice, and then he said, embarrassed, "I always sing along when I'm alone in my car."

"You're not really alone, though," I pointed out.

He blushed a little and bit his lip. "I guess not."

And then, "HOOOONK!!!"

"Thanks, Victor," Justin said, smiling through gritted teeth.

"Just getting you back for the popcorn comment." Everyone laughed.

Singing to Justin today was the first time I have sung in almost two weeks. And even though it was The Doors, it still felt really good. So good that I wish I could do it again. There's no way I could sing in my room here, though, without some adult running in and telling me to be quiet. I love the irony of the Quiet Room: It's the only room in this whole place where people are allowed to be loud.

AFTER DINNER

As Lawrence is on permanent room restriction for hitting Eugene, he never comes down to dinner. This is good because it gives the rest of us plenty of time to talk about him.

Troy, who has finally been let out of his hallway desk, had some insight since he shares a room with Lawrence. "The guy's a freak. And he reeks. Hey, that rhymes." OOOK. Profound words from one of the great minds of the twenty-first century.

"Isn't anyone else just a little afraid of him?" I asked.

"I am," Colby answered, but we all knew that already. "What if he eats Morgan?"

"Morgan's just a doll," Matt O. answered.

"And a plastic one at that. Do satanists eat plastic dolls? I didn't know that was part of their belief system." I couldn't help but crack a smile. The thought of Lawrence sitting down at a table with a fork and knife, checkered napkin tucked into his shirt, carving a plastic doll, was too genius.

And speaking of genius, "What's everyone talking about?"

I should probably mention that Callie was eating with us. She was definitely toned down from the skankiness presented when she first arrived. Her clothes were still tight, which should have bothered me, except that she was wearing giant white leather high-tops. So sick. When I saw those I knew she couldn't possibly be an All Star–wearing girl like Justin's type. Besides, Justin hasn't looked at or said a word to her since we got here, unless he did in Group when I wasn't around. What if he professed his love to her, and I don't even know it? Coincidentally, her presence also explains why there haven't been any elevator innuendo stories to tell. Now that there are several girls who can ride in the elevator, we ride separately from the boys. Isn't that illegal? I mean, segregation and all.

And isn't it interesting how the smallest details can make or break a person's attractiveness factor? For example, Troy was totally hot to me when I first got to the hospital, but the second he gave himself white-boy dreads, I lost all interest. That, plus the fact that the reason he's here is because he started a white supremacist group at his school after his black girlfriend dumped him. What I don't get is why then would he want white-boy dreads? Maybe that's part of his treatment: getting back to his roots. Or his ex-girlfriend's roots.

Callie, who I assumed was going to be the floor hottie with her perfect bod and general hoochiness, turned out to be a generic dud with hideous footwear. Never mind the fact that, according to our town gossip, Matt O., Callie's a klepto and a compulsive liar. I better keep an eye on my eraser-less pencils. One never knows when a lying klepto may strike. I'm trying to assume that Justin has the same negative opinion that I do, but what if he really wasn't looking at her or talking to her because he was playing hard to get and at night he has wet dreams about her? I think I will forever be traumatized by sex ed movies.

AFTER FREE TIME

Tra-la-la! Tonight I played Hearts with Justin, Matt O., and Sandy. Morgan just watched. I am getting quite good at the game. I watched Justin's scarred hand as he dealt the cards. I wonder if he'll ever tell me what happened.

Sandy is terrible at cards, since every time she tries to concentrate she has to lay Morgan on the table. Then Eugene or Bettina sees her and tells her that's no way to treat a baby, and she has to forfeit.

Tonight the TV was on, Sean's choice, and he watched a nature program about lions. I wasn't facing the TV, but Sandy was. Every time a lion did something she thought was gross, like rip apart a gazelle or have sex, she would wince and cover Morgan's plastic eyes. I faced the other end of the Day Room, where Phil, Callie, and Troy sat. It was darker over there, and I began to notice a proximity discrepancy. That is to say: Troy and Callie were touching. Phil, of course, was watching. It was very subtle, which I think is why it took everybody a while to catch on. Callie and Troy kept their eyes on the TV, but I watched as their hands slowly crept towards one another's legs. I think we got through two rounds of Hearts before they made actual contact.

Justin noticed me. "What are you looking at?"

"Don't turn your head," I said. "Callie and Troy are getting it on in the corner."

"What?" And he automatically turned. "They're not 'getting it on,' " he said.

"I know. I just wanted to say 'getting it on.' But they *are* touching."

He looked again. "Hmmm," he turned to me. "Whose turn is it to deal?"

Justin wasn't interested, but I still was. I was amazed that for some people it is just so natural to be sexy and sexual and rebellious. I am so not able to be any of those things. God, I could have sat next to Justin for a hundred years, and I would never have gotten the nerve to even assume he would want to touch me. But there they were, having known each other only two days, and not even having an opportunity to talk or plan to hook up, and they were just groping away in the corner. Does that make me immature, or just a total feeb? When I finally become "mature" will I just know how to kiss and know when a guy likes me and know where to touch him and when?

And then I felt something. It was on my shoe. At first I thought I was kicking a table leg, which always happens with my big feet. But I wasn't moving my foot, and something was moving against my shoe. First the front rubber part was tapped, and then there was definite friction along the side of the shoe. And then I felt a pant leg against my pant leg (or is it pants leg? Oh, who cares at this point!). We were still in the middle of a card game, but I knew who it was. The shoe being rubbed was my left shoe, and on my left sat Justin. The movement, the touching, was so slow that I didn't think anyone else noticed. I began to move my leg farther out and farther left, so he knew I was reciprocating. Slowly, slowly he crossed his foot over mine, and our legs locked. We would never have gotten away with holding hands at Lake Shit, so there we were, holding legs. Matt O. won the game. "Man, you guys bit that game!" And then, "Holy shit!" We all turned to see what he saw. Callie and Troy were seriously making out, with Phil just chuckling and watching. In two seconds, Eugene yanked Troy off of Callie and dragged him into the hallway. Quickly, Justin and I unhooked our legs. Bettina yelled, "Free Time's over. Go back to your rooms. Callie, come with me." Somberly we all walked back to our rooms. I wanted to grab Justin's pinky like he did to me once, to let him know how much I enjoyed being with him, but I was afraid if I did, someone would see and they would separate us like Callie and Troy. I wonder if I'll ever get to touch Justin the way Callie and Troy touched each other. God. I wonder if I'll ever be allowed to touch anyone ever again.

AFTER RELAXATION

Tonight was hilariously unrelaxing. I placed my pillow gently, ever so gently, on the floor. The music of choice for the evening was the smooth sound of Michael Bolton. Nast.

There we were, pretending to be relaxed, while all I could think about was the hair on Justin's face and the feeling of his pant leg. Sandy was next to me, with Morgan, of course. Tanya was there, and Callie and Abby. It was a regular girls' slumber party, without the actual slumbering or even the hint of a party. The music was blaring away, "*Bwa-wa-wa.*" Groan. Then someone in the room played a horn of their own. *Tooooot!* If you know what I mean. And if you don't—someone farted.

Callie sat up quickly and was like, "What? You guys say anything, and I'll kick your ass!" It was so funny that we were rolling on the floor laughing. Even Flora was laughing hysterically. I wonder how Troy will feel when he learns his woman can't control her gas.

Thursday, Day 14

AFTER BREAKFAST

Weird. You know how Callie said not to tell anyone about her unexpected expellation yesterday? I don't know who told, but all of the boys were giggling about it at breakfast. Callie didn't eat anything, and Troy tried to console her. "It's OK, baby, it's OK," like some tragedy happened. This was the proof to what I have already told you: No one forgets a farter. What's so wondrously wonderful is that the farter wasn't me. At least not this time . . .

In other news, Troy reported that this morning, instead of his newly reformed praying to God, Lawrence was back to praying to Satan. "That God shit wasn't working for him. I mean, Abby wasn't going for it, so he gave up on it. So it's all your fault, Abby, if he kills me in my sleep."

"Huh? What? Nuh-uh," was all Abby managed to spit out, along with some sprays of Cocoa Puffs.

"Hey, Abby," Phil asked, "how come you haven't had a seizure since you've been here? I want to see you talk like the devil!"

"Shut up, Phil. I don't choose when I have a seizure. It just, like, happens."

"Well, just let me know if you think you're gonna have one so I can come watch."

Nice. I really hope she never has a seizure when I'm around. I've never seen anyone have a seizure. I wouldn't know what to do. They haven't prepared us here either. Even if they did and Abby has a seizure, and I'm expected to help her, what if I can't? To tell you the truth, remember when we were both signed up for a CPR course last summer? And I called you and told you I had diarrhea and couldn't go? The truth is that I chickened out.

I was afraid that if I learned how to do CPR and then I was in a situation where I was expected to use it, I would screw it up and make a person die. I know—totally irrational, since trying would be better than not trying and knowing would be better than not knowing. But it's someone else's life, you know? Back to Abby—I just hope that someone in this hospital is actually trained in medicine and not just on how to prevent kids from touching each other.

It would be kind of weird if Abby doesn't have one of her seizures while she's here. My panic attacks (knock on wood, as my mom always says) have almost stopped completely. Colby hasn't heard any voices lately (as far as I know), and Abby . . . Could the medications they have us on be working? Or has being taken out of our normal life context changed us completely? What happens when we go back?

AFTER SCHOOL (SPECIAL!)

School was so lovey-dovey today. The "teacher" let Justin show me some of the blueprints he drew for an architecture class he has at real school. We sat next to each other on a bench, our jean-covered thighs touching. He leaned over numerous times to point things out, and every time he did I inhaled him. I think I was giving off some sort of hormonal force field, because the teacher told me it was time to go back to my own desk.

It's times like those when I just want to scream my head off to some really loud music. Punk. Cheesy '80s metal. I'd even blast

The Doors. I need to get out all of this pent-up . . . aggression? Tension? Lust? I'm going crazy! I mean, I have obviously liked guys before (see: The Erik Johnson Debacle), but nothing was ever tangible (in the abstract sense, of course). The actuality of it all is so intense! I can't get close to Justin anymore. I want us to touch *so badly.* My desire is so overwhelming I'm sure people can see it emanating from my body. Why oh why can't we have music here to help relieve the pressure? Why can't I sing when I want to? I must get it out or I will explode!

MINUTES LATER . . .

I have a plan. I'm going to get myself into the Quiet Room. If I get myself into the Quiet Room then I can sing anything I want as loudly as I want to. With the floor so small and the walls so thin, it's just known and accepted that if you go into the Quiet Room you turn into a wild, raging performer for the whole floor. That's what I have to do. But how will I get in?

AFTER LUNCH

Some regular Quiet Room customers are acting as my advisors on my new plan. Matt O. suggested running down the halls naked. He figured that'd be good for at least a couple of hours in the QR, but I figured he just wanted to see a naked girl (especially after being locked up for six months. I wonder if he's seen a naked girl before?). Troy suggested I hit Abby over the head with a chair, but I thought that might cause me to be confined to a desk in the hall again. Not to mention I've never hit anyone in the head with a chair. Or without a chair. Oy.

"I don't want to actually get in trouble," I said. "I just want to go to the Quiet Room."

"What's so bad about getting in trouble?" Troy asked.

I couldn't tell him the real reasons I didn't want to get in trouble. It's embarrassing to tell a group of kids who hit people and escape from boarding school that I've never gotten in trouble a day in my life, and I'm too afraid to start now. So I said, "I don't want to have to eat lunch in my room or in the hall. They never bring up the good food." Which was sort of true, although the real reason I didn't want to miss meals was because then I'd also be missing Justin.

"What about asking?" That was Justin's suggestion. "Maybe they'd let you go in if you asked."

Hmmm. Beautiful and brilliant. I think I'll try it.

AFTER GROUP

Group gets more and more useless the longer I am here. We never really talk about our families or our problems from home. It's always about some issue we're having at Lake Shit, like Eugene explaining why the No Touching rule is so important now that there has been a "breach," as he called it. In order to get points, we're supposed to say how the incident with Callie and Troy made us feel. But it's not like we could tell the truth and get any points. There was no way that if I said, "Seeing Callie and

Troy made me kind of jealous and made me want to do the exact same thing with Justin, and I think the rule sucks," that I would've gotten any points. I don't know how anyone around here gets enough points to make it to Level III. Except for Matt O. Did I tell you he is now a permanent Level III? Somehow his "doctor" decided that he needed more positive reinforcement, so every week he is the only Level III and gets to have a Friday night pizza party all by himself. If I could make it to Level III, I'd get a pizza party and a field trip. Matt O. only gets a field trip if there is another Level III to go with him. Pizza. Man, I miss pizza almost as much as I miss music. And a field trip? Actually leaving the building? I wonder if I would burn up from the contact with the sun.

The other discussion during Group today was that there have been a number of incidents lately that created a "violent air" to the floor. According to Eugene—and he looked right at Lawrence—"This needs to stop." Lawrence is such a total freak that he smiled a big, dark grin at Eugene. His gums showed, and I want to say they looked like my old German shepherd's gums, all black and slimy. I might be making that up, though.

FREE TIME

Free Time kind of sucked tonight. It was Sean's turn to choose TV stations [why is it always his turn?], and he put on *Full House* again. I don't get it: Is there a *Full House* channel that only mental hospitals subscribe to? Who else would? Phil/Shaggy watched the show and salivated at the Olsen twins because, as he put it,

"They are hot as hell now!" Um, maybe, but you're drooling over a pair of seven-year-olds at the moment. He should be locked up. Oh, wait—he is!

Because of the Callie and Troy incident, we were only allowed to socialize near members of the same sex. It was kind of funny because the rule only said "near," not "with," so Sandy, Matt O., Justin, and I attempted to play Hearts sitting across the room from each other. That didn't work, so Matt O. suggested, "Why don't we play catch with the doll."

"It's not a doll," Sandy smirked. "It's my baaaaaby." She sang the word "baby" in a cutesy voice and cuddled Morgan.

We decided to give up and watch the crap on TV.

About twenty minutes into Free Time, Bettina came into the Day Room. "Sandy? Sandy and Morgan?" Sandy raised her hand and called out, "Here." Bettina spoke as if she were reading the lines off of a teleprompter, "Morgan is crying very loudly and is interrupting everyone else's Free Time. Please take her back to your room so she does not disrupt Free Time." Robotically, Bettina left.

"At least you don't have to watch the rest of *Full House*," I said and shrugged. Sandy walked out of Free Time in misery, leaving me with the Olsen twins.

BEDTIME

I'm a little saddened by Sandy these days. She doesn't seem at all interested in taking care of Morgan. She used to tuck her into her bed at night, and whenever she did her homework Morgan sat next to her on her desk. Now she just puts Morgan on one of the shelves in the closet and closes the door whenever we're in our room. I asked her about it tonight.

"How come you don't hold Morgan anymore? What are you going to do when you have a real baby? I think you'd get arrested if you kept it in the closet." I was trying to be lighthearted.

"I don't know," she said, not looking at me. "I don't know what to do," and then she looked up at me, eyes all scared and trembly and wet.

I didn't know what to do either. This was so out of my reality, like from a TV show. Sex, pregnancy, plastic babies—isn't there supposed to be some doctor helping her through this? What if I say something wrong and she hates me for it? Or what if she listens to me and does something she regrets for the rest of her life, and it's all my fault?

I opened the closet door and held Morgan. "I can watch her for a little while, if you want."

"OK, thanks."

I looked into Morgan's fake dull eyes, laid down on top of my bedspread with Morgan on my chest, and pretended to read *The Crucible*.

Friday, Day 15
AFTER BREAKFAST

I talked again at breakfast about the Quiet Room. Justin still thought I should just ask them to go in. "The worst they can say is 'no.' " I've heard that saying before, but it never sounded as profound as when Justin said it. Justin. What the hell is going on with Justin and me? I feel like I'll never know. I mean, we're not allowed to touch and have relationships, and if either of us ever gets out of here someday (will we?), then what? It's not like we go to the same school or live in the same town. God. For all I know he doesn't even like me, and I'm just delusional from being locked up for two weeks. I wish there were some international sign of liking. Like, I like you, so I will now wave the symbolic flag of likehood. And let's just say Justin does like me. Does he like me because I'm the only girl (out of five) who is somewhat his type, and as long as we're locked up he'll take what he can get? But then he gets out of Lake Shit, goes home, gets a tall, skinny, big-boobed, blond girlfriend and forgets about me. It sounds like my odds are better off in a loony bin.

AFTER GROUP

Whoa, was I on a rampage today. First I bitched about boys and men and how women are expected to be a certain way, but we all can't possibly be that way so what the fuck?

"What happens if I never get thin and tall and perky? Does that mean that I am *wrong*? That I can never be *correct* unless I am that way? That absurd, gross, hard, angular way that all women are in the movies and TV?"

Victor piped up. "Hell no. I don't want some bony-ass bitch. Give me some soft, squishy goodness anytime." Why is it that the only guy I ever heard say he likes a chunky girl is locked up in a mental hospital? Maybe some of those guys who put anorexic freaks all over TV and magazines need to be locked up. And so do the anorexic freaks. Force-feed them a few Tater Tots and some Cap'n Crunch. I am so sick of feeling like shit just because I don't look like them.

That rant went on for almost the entire Group. I actually garnered some applause at the end from Abby, Victor, and Matt O. It's nice to know that some people agree with me about the unrealistic expectations thrust upon women's bodies, but it doesn't help me in knowing how Justin feels. And I'm still assless.

THE AFTER-LUNCH NEWS

Well, well, it seems our satanic troubles are finally over (some of them, at least). Lawrence has left the building. Actually, he's leaving this afternoon. According to Troy, "His parents want him to come home and help take care of his brothers and sisters." Can you imagine that freak taking care of little kids? I'm having trouble picturing him even having parents. I wish I could be there when they pick him up. His dad's probably eight feet tall with horns coming out of his head, and his mom's really skinny in a red leather bodysuit with a tail hanging off the back. It would be hilarious, though, if his mom is just a suburban soccer mom in a pastel suit and his dad is a businessman with slicked-back hair.

It should be interesting to see how he says goodbye to us.

When people leave here, they can either say goodbye in Group and Community, or write letters to people they want to say goodbye to. Hmmm . . . I have a feeling he'll choose letters so he doesn't have to deal with anyone. Eeew. What if he writes them in blood?

AFTER SCHOOL

I have been dissed! Double-dissed, in fact!

Diss #1: I asked Bettina really nicely if I could please have some time in the Quiet Room.

"What for?"

"I just want to go in there for a little while . . . you know . . . to be alone?" I felt totally retarded asking her, and I know I sounded all wimpy and suspicious.

"You gotta do something wrong to go into the Quiet Room, honey."

"Are you sure you couldn't just make an exception? I mean, I really need to go in there. Just for, like, ten minutes would be OK."

"Uh-uh," she said and walked away. Why am I such a goody-goody?

Diss #2: Lawrence did not leave me a goodbye note! Whatever! I was in his Group and put up with all of his faux evil bullshit, so what gives? And of course guess who got a note—Abby! I mean, the girl totally ignored his God-fearing advances, and he still cares enough to write her a note? I haven't seen the note yet, but Abby said she'd leave it in the bathroom for me to read. She said I should be glad to have not gotten a note from such a crazy freak, but at least it would have been something. I haven't even gotten one piece of mail since I got here. Doesn't anyone give a shit about me? I guess I shouldn't talk, since technically I haven't sent any of these letters to you. Yet. They are piling up on my desk, smearing a little because of the pencil. I don't have any envelopes or stamps, and I kind of like to see what I wrote about each day. It reminds me of how different things have gotten. I promise to give them to you when I get home, as long as the pencil hasn't smeared too much.

TRANSCRIPTION OF LAWRENCE'S EXIT NOTE TO ABBY
(TRANSCRIPTION DONE DURING STUDY TIME BY YOURS TRULY)

To My Dear Abby,

Although you were not willing to join me on my life's path, I want you to know that I am OK. I know my Lord Satan has plans for the two of us that will be revealed someday. You will come around. See you soon.

Luv,
Lawrence

Hee-hee. He signed the letter "luv." That's so hilarious and absurd. I guess I'm glad that he didn't write me a letter because in the back of my mind I would always be wondering how and where he would "see me soon."

AFTER FREE TIME

It's another second Friday night without a pizza party, since there were no Level IIIs (except for the poseur Level III that is Matt O.). It would be so cool if they told me I was Level III this Sunday (when they announce each week's levels) because then I'd get to enjoy the magical goodness that is pizza. Not to mention that if I were a Level III and no one else was, I would have complete control over the stereo and TV. No more *Full House* Channel! No more classic rock (except for The Doors, of course)!

Why am I in such a good mood, you ask? (Go ahead, ask me.) Justin and I had a wondrous conversation tonight. It turns out that Matt O., Justin's roommate, told him all about my rant in Group today.

"Matt told me what you said in Group today." Justin looked at me through his bangs while he, Matt O., Sandy, and I sat around a table playing Hearts. The proximity ban had ended for everyone except Troy and Callie.

"Oh yeah? Which part?" I was afraid that maybe I accidentally said something in Group about Justin and how *he* could never like someone like me, etc. I hoped I only *thought* that.

"About how women have all sorts of unrealistic expectations

about their bodies," Justin continued. "Matt and I were talking about how we totally agree with you. It sucks. I mean, look." Justin pointed to the TV, where some Victoria's Secret whores writhed their greasy bodies across the screen. "How's anybody supposed to compare to that?"

"*Why* is anybody supposed to compare to that?" I asked desperately.

"Nobody really is. It's an 'ideal' the media set for everyone."

"So you're saying that perfect fake bodies are ideal?"

"No, of course not. It's all just to sell more products. For instance, in Health class, in real school," Justin explained, "we learned all about how advertisers put subliminal messages in commercials."

"There's nothing subliminal about half-naked sluts on TV! I think that's pretty, um, liminal." I was angry and disappointed, but I was losing steam. I felt resigned to the fact that all guys, no matter how wonderful they may seem, are always going to be skank-lovers.

"No, I mean like in ads for alcohol, they show a glass with ice, and one of the cubes is in the shape of a naked woman. It's not something you notice unless you're looking for it, but your brain picks up on it and makes you think the drink is sexy or something."

"But now we're just back to what makes a naked woman sexy. Women are supposed to drink—"

Justin cut me off. "Anna, I'm not arguing with you. I'm agreeing with you. The media sucks. Unrealistic bodies suck. Big, floating breasts suck. At least, I think they do."

"I don't know if I agree with you on that one, buddy," Matt O. piped in. "I'd settle for one small, deflated breast at this point. When you've got nothing to compare them to, they all look good."

"Charming," I said to Matt O. To Justin, "I bet you say all that, but every girlfriend you've ever had has been skinny and perfect." I couldn't help myself.

"Every girlfriend? I've only had one, and she was short, and . . . Matt, what's that word you used the other night?"

"Juicy," he answered.

"Yeah. She was juicy."

And then Free Time was over. Do you know what this means? It means that not only is Justin capable of being attracted to non-skinny girls (the thought of him and an ex makes me gag just a little), but he and Matt O. talked about someone together and used the word "juicy." As you and I know, Matt O. told me I was juicy. Could that mean that there could actually have been a dialog between Matt O. and Justin, O Boy of My Dreams, which contained both my name and the word "juicy?" I think I am going to wet myself.

Saturday, Day 16

IN THE WEE HOURS OF THE MORN

On weekends they let us sleep in (ooh! 8:30!), but since we go to bed so early and I barely expend any energy in this place, I'm wide awake at 6:30.

Sometimes I just look at the walls in this room and feel like crap. I feel sad that I can't have my posters and magazine clippings and the rest of the junk in my bedroom at home. I feel sad that I have no choice but to lie on this bed (on top of the covers, of course) and stay in this room until I'm told to leave. But I also feel sad that I am kind of happy and comfortable here. I have friends, a nice roommate, and a gorgeous boy who possibly likes me, stuff planned for me to do every day so I don't even have to think, no parents making me feel like I'm their crazy little disappointment. I'm sad that I may have to leave someday. What if my life can't be this normal in the real world?

BREAKFAST

This morning Bobby and Phil/Shaggy played a game to see how many times they could go back to the lunch counter for a new box of cereal without getting caught. Phil only managed three boxes before the lunch lady (breakfast lady?) told him he'd had enough. If he hadn't been snickering like a hyena and over-exaggerated his sneaking, he probably would've managed at least one more box. Plus, I have a feeling that his choice of muesli ("It keeps me regular," he insisted) was what gave him away. Usually only the old people eat the muesli, and Phil was depleting their source. Bobby stuck to a more juvenile cereal, Apple Jacks, and managed to scam five boxes by way of his youthful charm. "I'm a growing boy," he pleaded to the lunch lady as she made him sit down. True loony bin excitement.

"I talked to my parents last night, and they said I get to go home soon," Bobby told us between slurps of his cereal. "They're going to let me go to Step."

"What's Step?" I asked.

"It's a school for kids with BD."

"What's BD?" Everyone looked at me like I was an idiot for asking this.

"Behavior disorders, duh." Oh yeah. "That way I won't be the only one who can't sit still. And the teachers won't get so mad at me. I hope."

I hoped so, too. Poor little growing boy.

ROTATION

This weekend we attended something new called "Rotation," where we sat opposite a person, talked to them for three minutes, and then switched. It seemed oddly social for this place, not to mention a lot like that speed dating I've seen on TV. The worst part about it was that I was forced to have three-minute conversations with people I don't normally enjoy talking with. Picture me sitting with Tanya for three minutes, asking her questions like, "How do you like being Abby's roommate?" and "What did you think of that breakfast game?" and Tanya just sitting there looking at her nails. She didn't say a single word to me. How rude! (Oh GOD! Did I pick that line up from *Full House*? Is that crappy show working its way into my subconscious? Soon

I'll be saying, "You got it, dude" and thinking Uncle Jesse's mullet is cool!)

I was also forced to sit with Phil/Shaggy for three minutes, which felt like a perved-out eternity. He kept asking me questions like, "So, do you have a boyfriend? Why not? What would you do with him if you did?" I tried to change the focus and asked Phil questions about home and school. "I don't remember," was the only answer he gave. Then he went on to ask what size bra I wore.

The good—no, great—no, wonderful!—part of Rotation was that I got to talk a whole three minutes with Justin. That was the first time we ever really got to talk without anyone else being in the conversation or monitoring us.

When we sat down, we were both silent for a few seconds. Then we started talking at once, stopped, started, stopped, and then both said, "You go first," and laughed. Finally I said, "I'll go first." I wanted to make sure we were kosher (I have always heard that word used to mean "OK," but I have never used it myself unless referring to hot dogs). It wasn't often that I opened myself up and shared my feminist views. Can I still be considered a feminist if I'm sucked into the body image bullshit? I have often wondered if the only people who can defend women's bodies are beautiful, thin, perfect women. My fear is that I'll talk about the unrealistic standards for women, and when I'm done some asshole will blurt out, "You're only saying that because you're fat and no one likes you." I said to Justin, "I hope I didn't freak you out yesterday with my diatribe."

"You didn't. Don't worry. I wasn't lying when I said I agreed with you. Not everyone watches those people on TV and thinks they're hot. How can I when they look so fake?" His hands were on his knees, which bounced up and down as he emphasized his ever-intriguing point. "Like, they're making all of these pouty faces and they're groping walls. Why am I supposed to think that's sexy again? Plus, not to be graphic, but the whole idea of touching a fake breast makes me think of squeezing a big ball of tapioca. And tapioca grosses me out."

"Ohmigod! Me, too!" I blurted. "That bubble tea they sell now? That's so sick! It looks like little fish eggs or balls of fat."

He laughed. I couldn't believe it. I had no idea that a guy could see past the long legs and cleavage to an actual person. Not to mention how gorgeous he looked as he talked about it.

"You know what else I hate?"

"Enlighten me," he said with a sly smile.

"I hate that face that all models and actresses make in photographs where their mouths are closed and not smiling, but you can just see their two front teeth. What's that about? It's so unnatural. I've tried doing it in the mirror, but it's hard. Maybe that's how you become famous. There's a test where they make you do all of these stupid poses and say stupid things, and the very last piece is where they take your picture, and if you can make the front tooth non-smile pose then you're in."

Justin laughed, and we both tried to make the face for the remaining twenty seconds of our time. When someone yelled "Switch!" Justin broke into a full, toothy smile, lifted his right hand, and gave a small wave. " 'Bye."

Shit. That would have been the perfect time to ask him about his hand.

STUDY TIME

Ugh. *The Crucible*. There has been no improvement to this tale of blandness. How could everyone in Salem be that utterly retardo? And the girls, excuse me, the "witches," are so lame. I wish they'd turn all *The Craft* and start doing evil things to the townsfolk who'd done them wrong. Or at least they could go *Charmed* and dress like skank-ho witches.

Tired of reading, I looked out the window with Sandy. The pastel getaway cars were still there. How could someone leave such funky cars in such a yucky parking lot? If I had either of them, I'd want to be seen in it driving around the city. Maybe whoever they belong to has a bunch more cars, even cooler than those, and felt like they didn't need the pink and blue ones around. Or maybe pastel cars are just too much trouble. Maybe it was easier for whoever owned them to just leave them in a parking lot across the street from us.

AFTERNOON

Who the hell is running this freak stand? Today our afternoon movie was the "classic" '80s flick *The Boy Who Could Fly*. Do you know this movie? You should, since they rerun it on UPN just about every Sunday. If not, here's a refresher: A mentally challenged boy (played by some guy named Jay Underwood, but whom I prefer to call Jay Underwear) lives next door to this boring girl. The boring girl has a brother and a mother, but no father because he killed himself when he found out he had cancer. The mentally challenged boy next door is always on the roof pretending he can fly. He actually believes he can, but no one else does. Until one day he and the boring girl are forced to jump off of a roof together and wheeeeee! They can fly! And, eeew, there was this totally gross kiss at the end between the boring girl and the mentally challenged flying boy. This movie was, like, directly out of the handbook on what *not* to show at a mental hospital. First of all, way to go, Dad! Not only did you just give up, but you killed yourself! And mentally challenged flying boy? What kind of lesson is this supposed to teach us exactly? I hardly think it wise to put the idea of flying into the heads of impressionable teenagers who are already battling the challenges of lunacy.

AFTER DINNER

I spoke with the floor again about getting into the Quiet Room. How can I be expected to get along for over two weeks without shouting out at least one Descendents' tune? While everyone theorized on the best way to get into the Quiet Room without getting in trouble, I thought more about the motives of the adults in this place. I know I'm always joking about how absurd everything is here, but the truth is that most of the things they make us do or tell us not to do don't make sense. If anything, being locked up here just makes me feel more disassociated with the real world. Maybe I couldn't sit inside of a movie theater or a classroom without freaking before I came here, but what exactly have they done for me in Lake Shit that is going to fix my panic attacks when I leave? What if they just start right back up again? If I want to sing, I should be allowed to sing—*encouraged* to sing for my well-being! The fact that they said no, I couldn't go into the Quiet Room just because I wanted to, pisses me off! I seriously don't know if these people, these "grown-ups," want to help me or if they just want to make their lives as easy as possible. Sounds like some other adults I know . . . Isn't that the reason I'm here in the first place? Because my crappy therapist couldn't fix me, and my parents had already pawned me off onto the crappy therapist. Easier to just send me away and hope I come home all better. Must be nice having the luxury to deal or not deal with a person.

"Why don't you just break something?" Victor suggested. "That way you don't gotta hurt nobody, but you still got a ticket in."

"I find that high-pitched screams work well." Bobby had already been in the Quiet Room twice for this.

"I'm tellin' ya, just ask them." As fine as Justin is, his pacifism was wearing on me.

"I already tried that. They don't care that I need to go in. I'm thinking of taking drastic measures."

"Like what?"

"I'm not sure yet. I've never taken drastic measures. I just like how it sounds."

"If you do something bad you might not get to Level Three," Justin reminded me.

"Nobody ever gets to Level Three, except for the almighty Matt O.! I don't know if I even believe in Level Three. It's probably just something the staff made up to make us behave like little robots and stick our stupid fingers out and sit in farty chairs and drink juice that makes us even more thirsty than before we started drinking!"

"Good thing you're in a mental hospital, 'cause you're sounding a little crazy," Bobby said.

He was right. I did sound crazy. But crazy is sometimes good. I mean, you can be crazy in love, right? Crazy about the Cubs. Crazy for yellow cupcakes with frosting and colored sprinkles (mmmmm). Maybe crazy is what I need to make things actually happen in my life.

SATURDAY NIGHT—WITH FEVER

Give me a break! Bettina and Eugene are now telling Sandy that Morgan's sick and that she keeps pooping in her diaper and crying.

They came into our room every five minutes for the first hour of her as-yet-unnamed illness and told Sandy to change her diaper. Then they said they weren't going to come in anymore, but Sandy better keep changing her diaper every five minutes 'cause there were going to be surprise checks. I'm so sure. They only stopped coming in because they didn't want to move. What I want to know is, who's paying for those diapers? Are they charging Sandy's insurance for that? And what a waste! I heard that the #1 thing polluting our world's landfills is diapers. There's not even poop in there!

"Maybe you should just use the same diaper over and over again," I told Sandy.

"Yeah, I guess," she said wearily.

"What's wrong?"

"What's wrong? I'm sixteen years old. I'm pregnant. I'm locked in a mental hospital with my plastic black baby, and I'm going to get fat from all of this eating. . . ." She trailed off as tears started falling. "My doctor's still talking about abortion." Sandy curled up on her bed around Morgan.

What will Sandy's life be like if she has an abortion? If she doesn't? I just think about what if I believed that an abortion was killing a human being, and then I had one and I felt like I was killing my own baby? Is that how she would feel?

Sunday, Day 17

Sundays always suck. Maybe it's the fact that we've been taught since childhood that Sundays are the end of the weekend.

I don't know why it should feel different than any other day here, but it does. They don't keep us as busy on Sundays, and instead of actually seeing the people we want to see in activities, we're stuck most of the day in our rooms. Not that I mind spending time with Sandy, it's just that she's been so mopey and quiet lately. I'm sure she's stressed about the baby decision. I decided to try and cheer her up.

"Wanna play a game?"

"Nah."

"Draw portraits?"

"Nah."

"Look at the getaway cars and plan our escape?"

"OK." We walked to the window. Already darkened by the screen, the sky looked unfriendly. "The cars are still there," Sandy noted, even though I could see them myself.

"Which one do you want?" she asked.

"I hadn't thought about it. I assumed we'd escape together, in the same car."

"So which car should we take? I'm pretty partial to the pink one," I said. "It's so Barbie. Plus, maybe people will think we sell Mary Kaye cosmetics."

"What do you mean?"

"Haven't you heard of that? There's some makeup company where women sell products door-to-door, and the more they sell, the more pink stuff they win. If they sell a ton, they get a pink car. I saw a made-for-TV movie about it."

I really hope we don't manage to escape. What would I do? On the lam with a pregnant sixteen-year-old? That's so not me. And if we left, what would happen to everyone at Lake Shit? Everyone pretty much being Justin, of course. I could probably come back here in five years and still find Matt O., but if I leave without knowing how Justin feels about me or what happened to his hand or even how to get in touch with him once we're home, then that's it.

Good thing I'm such a wuss.

AFTER LUNCH

Lunch today was as soggy as the weather. People didn't talk much, and even the food looked gray.

"What movie are we watching tonight?" I asked.

"The nine-billionth *Star Wars*," Matt O. said. "No shit. I've been here six months, and every Sunday they show one of the *Star Wars* movies. I'm so sick of them. I'd even settle for that flying boy movie again."

"You would?"

"No. Not really. That was way off."

"I don't care what movie they show, as long as the lights are off," Troy said and smiled slyly at Callie. One would think that the adults in this place would have some memory of the make-out scandal of last week, but after a few days, Callie and Troy were sitting next to each other again. I can only imagine what base they could get up to in the dark of a movie. Did I just say base? That is soooo middle school. And you know what's sad? I never even knew what the bases stood for. These are my guesses:

1st Base: lip kiss
2nd Base: touching over clothes
3rd Base: touching under clothes
Home Run: full-on doing it, plus some other things that I've heard about, but feel weird writing down.

Is that right? Oh god. I cannot imagine ever ever ever being naked with another human being in my whole life. Is it ever going to happen? Do I want it to happen? Will I know what to do if it does? Maybe I should keep an eye on Callie and Troy for some pointers. Would that make me a Phil-level perv? Hey—I know! I'll get a boyfriend who can show me how to do everything! Yeah! That sounds so easy, why didn't I think of it sooner? Oh wait—I did. Like, every single second of my life. I am getting very desperate here.

PET THERAPY

What a pathetic loser I am. The hospital brought in animals today as a way to make us feel good, and not a single animal came near me. There were puppies and kittens and dogs and cats and even a bunny, and not one liked me. I sat on the floor next to Justin and Matt O., and all of the animals passed me and went directly to one of them. Matt O. had particular luck with the dogs, which he attributed to the fact that his special mental hospital plan does not require him to bathe every day and he had acquired a somewhat ripe scent. The animals looked so cute and soft, and I called to them in the nicest of ways, but they ignored me. One dog smelled my shoe, looked totally disgusted, and walked over to Justin instead. Hello—we have the same shoes! Does that say something about me? If animals don't like you, doesn't that mean you're a serial killer? No, that's if you murder animals, which I have to admit I kind of wanted to after none of them wanted to talk to me. Does that make me a serial killer? The ironic thing is that the animals were supposed to be here to make us feel happy and loved, and instead they just made me feel crappy and lonely. Maybe it meant that I smelled good, though, since they were attracted to the foul-smelling Matt O., and they do have a tendency to sniff each other's butts. How is this therapy again?

COMMUNITY ROCKS!

You will never guess what happened to me in Community. No, I didn't make out with Justin while everyone gave us points. I got into Level III! Eugene said he really liked how I expressed myself in Group and thought I was getting my act together nicely. I guess he's referring to how in Group when someone else has something to say, I usually constructively give advice, like, "Colby, I think it would be perfectly OK for you to talk to the voices in your head, as long as it doesn't wake up anyone else." Or when people get into shouting matches, like the time Phil/Shaggy and Sean got into a shouting match over how much beer you have to drink to make yourself pass out, I don't join in screaming like everyone else (perhaps because I've never had beer?). Whatever the official reasons are for getting me on Level III, I'm pretty stoked. Not only will I have complete control over the TV and radio, but I get to go on a field trip and have a Friday night pizza party! And now for the best news of all: Guess who else made it to Level III . . . Correct! Justin! That means we can choose radio stations together! We can feed each other pizza on Friday night! Greatest and most fantastic of all is that we get to go outside of the mental hospital into the real world! Together!

SNACK TIME

Raisins again. I like raisins, but I have a habit of losing one or two on the floor every time I eat them. I always find them later and think they are: a) a mouse turd or b) a cockroach. Then I figure out it's a raisin and sigh with relief. This pretty much happens every time I find a lost raisin.

BEDTIME

I've been thinking. While I'm beyond the world of thrilled that Justin and I get to share Level III with each other (It kind of makes us like the mental hospital royalty, doesn't it?), it's weird to think about the fact that I got to Level III. I mean, of course I did. When don't I do everything I'm told to do? I'm in a mental hospital, which means I'm supposed to be a total fuckup, and what do I do? I play nice, I don't touch anyone, and I follow all of the rules. I feel like such a spaz. I wish I had the balls to break something or swear at someone or just not do what I'm supposed to do. I'm completely afraid that if I mess up, people won't like me. But *I* still like the people who are getting in trouble (for the most part). Matt O. is always in and out of the Quiet Room, and he's one of my favorite people here. Plus, I don't really like the people who are giving out the punishments, so why do I care what they think of me? Is this how rebels think? Are they better than us wimpy people because they don't care what other people think? Or are they worse because they don't care if they hurt people? Or are they neither because nobody is all one way all of the time anyway? I have no answers, only questions as usual.

As a Level III, I have to wonder what the adults think they're doing for us. I can see that a lot of us are "better"—without panic attacks, satanic possession, swastikas—but will this apply in the real world? All we do is talk about the problems we're having here. I am going to be a bigger freak in the real world when I go back to school (yikes!) and stick my fingers out instead of raising my hand. What if someday I'm back home and I get a real boyfriend and I'm afraid to touch him? What if I can't ever fall asleep again without first listening to shitty music? Maybe I'd be better off living here forever.

Monday, Day 18

AFTER BREAKFAST

Sandy wasn't at breakfast today. She said she had an appointment with her doctor, which was weird because it was so early.

At breakfast Victor proposed a toast: "To Anna and Justin [Our names sound so good together, don't they?] for making it to Level Three!" Everyone cheered their milk cartons and juice cups together. "Let's hope they make it somewhere else, too!" He winked. Cheers to that!

TEN MINUTES LATER, STILL IN ROOM

Sandy hasn't come back to our room yet. It's strangely lonely in here without her. It reminds me of being in my bedroom at home, happy to be by myself but wishing I had someone to be with. It wouldn't be so bad in here if it weren't so creepy quiet. Quiet isn't always bad, but it's nice when you at least have some control over it.

AFTER GROUP

Abby had a seizure! Abby had a seizure! It was so weird. One minute, Phil/Shaggy was talking out of his ass about the gang he used to sell drugs for (yeah, right), and the next minute Abby was flopping around on the floor like a fish. I don't mean to sound insensitive (which is basically saying that I do), but that's really the best way to describe it. Her eyes rolled, her mouth hung open, and her arms and legs jerked up and down. It felt like there were a solid thirty seconds where everyone just stared at her, waiting for Satan to speak out of her mouth. That's what I was waiting for, at least. But when she didn't speak and she just kept flopping, Eugene, Bobby, and Matt O. got onto their knees and tried to help her. Eugene pulled out a walkie-talkie and called for medical help. I didn't want to stare at Abby because that seemed rude, and I didn't want to look at anyone else because that seemed creepy, so I just stared into a corner until help arrived.

I couldn't believe how Matt O. took control of the situation. He hasn't touched anyone in six months, and there he was holding on to Abby during her seizure. And there I was, afraid to look at her, afraid to touch her, afraid to look at anyone.

When I got back to my room after Group, Sandy was finally there. She stood at the window, fingers pressed against the screen.

"You OK?" I asked. She pulled her hands off of the screen, and itty-bitty squares dotted her fingertips like new fingerprints.

"I'm fine," she said. I could tell she was lying. "What happened in Group? We heard a lot of yelling."

I told her about Abby and how I was freaked. "Did she talk like the girl in *The Exorcist?*"

"No. It was scary enough without that. I would have heaved all over if she went devil-child on us. I wonder if any of that was even real. The seizure looked real, not that I've ever seen a seizure before, so I don't think she was faking. Why would she fake it?"

"So people don't think she's a liar."

"I think if she was really lying she would have faked a little devil talk, like, 'Let Abby go. Satan warns you.' You know, so she could get out of here."

Sandy looked at me while she chewed her lip.

"I don't think it quite works that way," she said.

"What works what way?" There were too many thoughts and memories rushing through my brain to sort out what she was referring to.

"Lying, I mean. I don't think lying's the best way to get out of here."

Sandy picked at a loose piece of skin on her finger. I waited. "Sometimes," she continued, "lying is what gets you here in the first place." She spoke slowly and apologetically.

"What are you talking about?" I hated feeling naïve.

"I'm not pregnant." She smiled fakely, eyebrows raised.

"Did you lose the baby?" I still didn't know what she was talking about.

"Not exactly. Not at all, really. I was never pregnant."

Say what now?

"I faked it so Derek wouldn't break up with me. Again."

This is so Jerry Springer! "You pretended that you were pregnant so your boyfriend would think he had to be with you forever? What did you think would happen when no baby came out?" I was pissed, mostly because she lied to *me.*

"I just figured by that time he would be so in love with me again that it wouldn't matter. That's what happened last time."

"Last time? You did this before?"

"Just once. I kind of *thought* I was pregnant at the time, until I got my period. But Derek was being so nice to me and buying me treats and mini Cubs T-shirts that I couldn't tell him the truth."

"So what did you tell him?" My anger was surpassed by the curiosity and disbelief of it all.

"I told him I lost the baby. At cheerleading practice. Everyone made a big deal over me after that, but then they forgot and Derek and I started getting in fights again. This just felt like the right thing to do."

I sat on my bed, dumbfounded. I was duped; I didn't know Sandy at all.

"I talked to Birdcage this morning and told him everything because I was so sick of changing Morgan's fake diaper, and feeding her fake face, and losing sleep over a stupid, fake baby." She whipped Morgan against the screen, and she dropped to the floor like the plastic doll she was.

"Birdcage said they already knew I wasn't pregnant because of all the blood and urine tests, and they just wanted to see how I'd handle the responsibility." That is so messed up. They knew? Maybe Birdcage thought it wasn't hurting anyone, since Derek isn't here and he probably told her parents. Did they even consider how it would affect those of us who are paying Lake Shit customers?

"Birdcage set up a phone call for me and Derek tonight, so

I can tell him." Sandy didn't seem bothered at all. "I can't wait to hear his voice. I hope he doesn't dump me."

I think she wanted me to say something reassuring, but what did I know about sex and boyfriends and fake pregnancies? I was pissed that someone I thought was on my side was just as full of shit as all of the assalong adults here. "I need to do some homework," I told her, and I lay back on my bed, not reading *The Crucible*.

AFTER LUNCH

Trying to ignore the Sandy betrayal sitch, I looked forward to my new QR final plan. I tell the workers that Abby's seizure messed me up and I really need to go into the Quiet Room to let off some steam. Then I can finally give my full twenty-four-minute rendition of the CD *The Ramones* by The Ramones. Brilliant.

Justin said he liked my plan and thought it would work. "Throw in a Doors tune for me if you remember." God, why don't I think that's dorky? I feel like such a softy because I know in the real world I would've been skeezed by a guy who only likes The Doors. I love how Justin, someone who likes The Doors, and me, someone who likes punk, can be friends (and I hope, someday, more than friends), and some funny black guy from a completely different social world and I can be friends, and even someone who's lived in a mental hospital for six months and I can be friends. Mental hospitals: bringing the world's cultures together through lunacy.

AFTERNOON

Mother F-ers! When I got back from school today, I stuck my fingers out of my bedroom door. I was all ready to give my rousing "Abby seizure" speech so I could jam in the Quiet Room, but it took someone, I swear, ten minutes to come to my door. It's so annoying because I know that either a) they couldn't see my fingers because we're not allowed to wave or call out or anything or b) they saw my fingers just fine, but they were too busy doing all the nothing that they always do to come over and see what I wanted. When Bettina finally came over, I said, "Um, I'm really freaked out because of Group today."

"What about Group?" Bettina scolded.

"Abby's seizure really freaked me out, and I need to go to the Quiet Room to, you know, let off some steam."

"Are you in trouble for something?"

"No, I just told you why I want to go."

"It doesn't matter. Being in the Quiet Room is for punishment only. If you go in there, we gotta supervise you, time it, and put it in your record. It's a lot of work for us. You just stay in your room. You'll feel better soon, I'm sure."

And that was it. Lazy turds. The whole reason they don't want me to go in is because it makes extra work for them? I need to sing so badly, but I can't do it in my room with Sandy moping on her bed. I was so ticked off at her for lying to me and so pissed at this hospital for trying to help me, so I snapped.

"Why did you lie to me?" I blurted out at Sandy.

"Lie to you? What do you mean?"

"What do I mean? You told me you were pregnant. You made me feel sorry for you. I helped take care of your 'baby'!" I used angry finger quotes.

"I'm sorry," she mumbled. "I didn't really think I was lying to you. I was lying to Derek."

"Derek isn't here! I thought you trusted me—that we were friends!" I was embarrassed to say this. It felt like the whole mental hospital popularity that I experienced was all in my head.

"We *are* friends. I thought if you knew the truth you wouldn't have any reason to like me."

"You thought I'd like you better with a baby? I have never had a friend with a baby! Not that I couldn't, but . . . There are a lot of things to like about you besides the fact that you can reproduce."

Sandy laughed. "Like what?"

I reminded her of all the games we played that she came up with. How funny she was. How skinny she was. How she actually made me look good in her portraits. "Those are friend things, not pregnant girl things."

"Oh," she smiled at me. "Thanks, Anna." She dragged Morgan off the floor and plopped down on my bed. "Can I interest you in a plastic babydoll with a dented head?"

"Not really." I took the doll and got up, opening our bedroom door quietly. I looked back at Sandy and then whipped Morgan as hard as I could down the hallway towards the check-in desk. Sandy and I bolted to our beds and pretended to read.

Instantly, Bettina opened our door. "Who threw this?"

Innocently, I said, "I don't know. She must have walked."

"But this is your baby," Bettina accused Sandy.

"She doesn't have a baby. Ask her doctor," I challenged.

"Young lady, come with me." Bettina pointed the doll at me.

THE QUIET ROOM

So I finally figured out how to get into the Quiet Room: throw a baby down a hallway and then talk back to an adult. Who knew it would be so easy? Or natural?

I followed Bettina next door to the Quiet Room. She unlocked the white door with one of the thousands of keys on her key ring. "One hour," she said. "Then I'll let you out." I walked inside, and she shut the heavy door behind me.

The Quiet Room wasn't exactly what I expected. The walls were white cinder blocks, not the padding I pictured. The floor was also white, and there were screened windows just like the ones in my room. The only object in the room was a large mirrored half-bubble on the ceiling with a camera inside.

I walked around slowly. Hesitantly, I spoke to myself to get used to the sound of my voice in such an enclosed room. "Well, here I am in the Quiet Room." My cautious words echoed slightly. I spoke the words again, louder. They bounced back to me. Forgetting about the camera, I yelled a primal scream from the bottom of my stomach. I waited. No one came in or knocked on the door. I was alone. I started to sing. I sang my heart out, loud and fast and screeching. Every time I finished one song, I thought of another that I'd been dying to hear for almost three weeks. I sang every song from beginning to end. I even played a little air guitar, but quickly stopped when I looked at the camera bubble. I felt kind of stupid, but amazingly free. I even felt a little *bad*. I did something wrong, and I was punished for it. GETTING IN TROUBLE was always this huge scary monster hanging over my head. Why? It turned out to be kind of fun. Maybe that's why the bad kids don't seem to care when they get in trouble. Really, it's not so bad at all.

In the middle of one of my favorite Ramones songs, I heard the door lock click. I stopped abruptly, and Bettina motioned for me to come out. She walked me back to my room, the silence echoing in my ears.

I slowly eased myself onto my bed. My arms and legs were sore from moving around so much and my throat felt raw, but I finally got to hear my music again. It was so worth it.

MONDAY AFTER DINNER

After congratulating me on my moving musical visit to the QR, Matt O. reported that he, Justin, and I would be visiting the Shedd Aquarium on our field trip this Thursday. That's so cool. I love field trips. Whenever we went on one during school in the real world, it was like everything changed. Every student and teacher looked and acted differently. Popular kids talked to the dorks, and the jocks talked to the punks. Bus rides and lunches were like another world. Teachers lost interest in the students and chatted the whole day with each other. They even fell asleep on the bus rides home. I don't know what the Shedd field trip will be like on Thursday, since there are only three of us. Will we even take a bus? How many chaperones will there be? Eeew—will Eugene go? Will we have to do some kind of special fish therapy? Ohmigod—what if they have us swim with the dolphins? Poor dolphins. It's so sad that they're trapped in Chicago and are forced to perform stupid dolphin tricks for measly rewards of fish. If we get to swim with them, I will do my best to set the dolphins free (although I don't think a bunch of dolphins would fare very well in Lake Michigan).

Speaking of freedom, the field trip will be my first time outside in twenty-one days. I wonder what it will feel like. Will I get instant sunburn because my skin isn't used to sunlight? What if I go blind? What if I start sweating profusely from a weird chemical reaction between the sunlight and my new armpit hair, and Justin thinks I'm a repulsive, sweaty pig? What if going back into the real world starts up my panic attacks? Ugh. Who would have thought a field trip could cause so much stress?

AFTER FREE TIME

Level III. This is the life. Justin and I sat on opposing green and yellow fart chairs next to the stereo. We decided it was fair for each of us to take turns tuning the radio dial until we found a station we both agreed on. We started low on the dial and worked our way upward. I would have liked to have found a cool college station, but Lake Shit doesn't get good reception and I wasn't sure if Justin would OK the obscure music they play. We passed adult contemporary (snore), slow jams (gag), and hip hop (shouts of "Leave it! Leave it!" from the rest of the Free Time crowd). Justin's finger stopped on the classic rock station, which seems to be the mental hospital standard. "How about this?" Justin looked eager. It was a Who song, I believe, which I could tolerate. I mean, as long as it wasn't a god-awful Eagles song that my dad used to force upon me as a child, it wasn't that bad. And how could I say no to that face? We didn't really talk the rest of Free Time but instead enjoyed being able to choose (sort of) and listen to music. Of course, I know it was the perfect opportunity to talk to him about his hand, but he looked chill. I didn't want it to look like the only thing I ever noticed about him was his hand. Besides, wouldn't he have told me about it already if he wanted me to know?

The only moment of Justin-and-Anna interaction came when that embarrassing song "Feel Like Makin' Love" came on the radio. I didn't know it was that particular song at first because it started out all acoustic and generic classic rock-y. But then it went all jammy, and the guy was yelling, "I feel like makin' love!" over and over, and finally added, ". . . to you!" So sick. I couldn't help but sneak looks at Justin every five seconds or so to see what his face looked like and if he was looking at me. I couldn't tell, though, because I didn't want to move my body and make it obvious, so I kind of just peeked at him from the corner of my eye at frequent intervals throughout the song. I hope he didn't think I was some leering freak. Or maybe he thought that I thought that whatever I was doing with my eyes was flirting, and he just pretended not to notice because it was not turning him on at all. Did he feel like making love? Would I ever know if I felt like making love? I glanced over at him so many times that I got a crazy headache and had to close my eyes. When Free Time ended, Justin and I got up, exchanged quick glances, and said, "Good night." Crap. Now he'll never feel like making love to me because he thinks I'm some creepy-eyed pervert. Do people actually say that anymore? Making love, I mean. What sounds better, though, "having sex?" "Getting nasty?" Never mind. Pretend I never wrote any of this. Justin would have to touch or kiss me or do anything before I ever have to think about what I'll call it, and that is not going to happen. When could it happen?

Maybe Justin is just shy, and maybe he can't tell if I like him because I'm sending him weird sideways glancing eye signals that he can't comprehend. What if somehow I make the first move? Not sex, of course, but what about trying to kiss him? What have I got to lose, except for my dignity, having to deal with the horrible pain and humiliation of rejection, and the pathetic knowledge that I may never actually kiss a human being in my entire life and that some guy in a mental hospital won't even kiss me . . . Plus, the fact that I'm too big a wuss to ever ask him about his hand, let alone kiss *him.* Will the pain never end?

BEDTIME

Snack tonight was pretty good—white chocolate–covered raisins. Sandy didn't want hers, which was different, since she'd been eating for two and more. I guess her acid-washed jeans were getting a little snug, and she wants to get back into shape for her reunion with clueless Derek. They talked on the phone for about five minutes tonight, and she came back beaming.

"He still loves me. He can't wait until I come home, and he's glad we won't have a baby to take care of."

"He wasn't mad at all?"

"Well, he kind of thinks it was another miscarriage." I rolled my eyes. "I won't do it again. I swear."

"As long as I don't have to be around when you do."

Even though Sandy was still lying, at least she wasn't lying to me. Plus, she was the only friend I had in the room with me for the next ten hours, and I really needed someone to talk to about Justin. I said, "I have to tell you about something."

"Don't tell me: You're pregnant!"

Was she kidding? "Um, hardly. But there is someone here I kind of like."

"Oh, I know. Justin. And I don't blame you. He's a real sweetheart."

Ohmigod! She knew? Was I that obvious? Did everyone know? Was I following him around like a roly-poly puppy? "How did you know?"

"Because he always smiles at you. Whenever I talk about you

in Group, nothing bad, of course, just when we're talking about roommates and stuff, he listens. And you guys sit by each other and . . ."

"Wait. Everything you just told me has to do with what *Justin* is doing." I was confused.

"Well, yeah. I just assumed it was mutual." Sandy shrugged.

"Mutual? As in I like him and he likes me?"

"That's what we're talking about, isn't it?" Sandy didn't get it.

"So what you're saying is, you think he likes me?"

I was waiting for a "maybe" or "possibly" or an "in your dreams," but Sandy said, "Totally." I was quietly taking in this bizarre fact, when Sandy asked, "Is that all you wanted to talk about? I want to fall asleep so I can dream about Derek."

I nodded, and she flicked off the lights.

This conversation was like a revelation. Not that it's really, truly official at this point ('cause what's the point of knowing someone likes you if you don't hear it from them), but if someone else with actual guy experience is noticing things, then maybe the things are really there.

Please, God, let me dream about Justin tonight.

Tuesday, Day 19
MORNING

For the first night in forever, I slept well. It was wonderful not having Morgan in here to wake us up. I did have a weird dream, though. Morgan was driving the pink getaway car while Sandy and I sat in the backseat eating Cap'n Crunch and singing "Feel Like Makin' Love." I wonder what Freud would say about that one.

AFTER GROUP—BOBBY'S GOODBYE

I felt a little sniffy as we said goodbye to Bobby in Group. Not that I knew him that well, but I liked having someone younger, sibling-ish, around.

He chose hugs for his goodbye. As we went around the group, each person had to say something nice about Bobby along with their hug.

Phil: "I'm going to miss our cereal challenges."

Matt O.: "You were fun to play cards with."

Colby: "I was never afraid of you."

Sean: "You always had lots of Band-Aids."

Tanya: "You didn't annoy me that much."

Me: "You reminded me of my little sister, but not in a girly way. Just because you're younger. And nice. I'll shut up now."

He gave me a young, weak hug, and Group was over.

I wonder what the goodbyes will be like when (if?) I get out.

BEDTIME

Watching Justin at dinnertime (I hope I didn't look like a drooly stalker) has convinced me that I have to do two things: 1. I must find out what the deal is with Justin's hand and 2. I am going to kiss Justin at the Shedd Aquarium. I figure it'll be the easiest place to do it because I'll be with him all day and probably under not as much supervision as normal, what with the slackness of adults on field trips. I'm sure my level will go down for next week anyway because of the baby-throwing incident, so even if I get caught and in trouble it won't really make a difference. Shit. I guess Justin will get in trouble, too, and if he doesn't want to be kissing me, then not only will I be dissed, but he'll be mad at me for lowering his Level. But if he does want to be kissing me, then he won't care, just like I won't care. Oh god. Even bigger problem: How do you kiss?

Wednesday, Day 20

BREAKFAST

Sandy and I had to eat in our room this morning because we're both scheduled to meet early with our doctors. I wonder what Dr. Asshole is going to say about my Quiet Room stay.

While we ate and waited, I thought it might be the right moment to ask her about something I was a little nervous about. I wasn't kidding last night about being clueless about kissing. I have no idea how. I mean, of course I know how to pucker and peck, but I was kind of hoping I'll get to use my tongue with Justin. The aquarium may be my only chance to ever kiss him, and I do not want to screw it up because of my ignorance in the realm of kissage. I decided to get Sandy's help with Operation Justin.

"So I've decided to make a move on Justin at the aquarium."

"That's so great! He seems kind of shy in Group, so I bet he's going to love that you're finally taking control."

"Really?" I felt a twinge of jealousy that Sandy knew a bit about Justin that I didn't. But I needed more info. "Are you sure he won't be grossed out?"

"Anna! Are you kidding? How could he possibly be grossed out by you? You're adorable!"

"I know, the adorable chubby girl." I hated how anyone who wasn't skinny had to be in the cute range of attractiveness, not the sexy range.

"I didn't mean it like that. I mean that you're so smart and funny and interesting and creative and, I am not just saying this, so pretty! He will totally be thrilled when you kiss him." Strangely, I kind of believed her at that moment. Now for the embarrassing part.

"Sandy?" I asked in a way that she knew I wanted something.

"Yeah?" she answered suspiciously.

"I need your help with something." I was not quite ready to get to the point.

"Like what?" she asked, imitating the slow way I kept asking her things.

"Well . . . how . . . exactly . . ."

"Uh-huh?"

"Do . . . you . . ."

"Oh god," she interrupted, "you're not going to ask me how to have sex, are you?"

"No!" I laughed, although it did freak me out that (hopefully) someday I would have to figure that out, too. "How do you kiss someone?" There. I got the question out. I would've asked you, of course, Tracy, but who knows when and if the letter would get out in time. I needed info *fast*.

"What do you mean? You just do."

Oy. I knew this would be difficult. I knew that it really was just natural for most people and I was just a freak of nature who was missing the make-out gene. "Um, like, but what do you do with your tongue? When do you use it? And how? And why do people in movies look like they're eating each other's mouths instead of giving kisses? And why do they move their heads so much?" The questions just kept coming. I felt like a kindergartner.

Sandy looked pensive. "Hmmm. I never really thought about it in those ways. Here. Make a fist." I closed my fingers tightly into my palm. "Not so hard. A soft fist. Now kiss it." Oh god. So embarrassing. What if they really do have surveillance cameras set up behind the light fixtures in our room? You know they're going to sell tapes of this to *America's Lame-Ass Home Videos*, or whatever that show is called.

I crept my mouth towards my hand and quickly gave it three fast, close-mouthed kisses. "There," I said, red and hot in my face.

"Real smooth," she laughed. "Try this." She softly opened her mouth a little and lightly wrapped her lips around her thumb several times. I tried it, and it felt OK. "Now add your tongue," she said. She rhythmically moved her tongue in and out of the mouth-hole she made on her hand, while at the same time moving her lips like she did before. I tried it, and after a while my hand was full of slobber.

"Is your hand all wet?" I asked.

"No," she answered. "Maybe you're using too much tongue. You don't have to french the whole time. Just sometimes, in the middle of everything." Check. Tongue during middle. Not whole time.

"What do I do with my hands?" I asked, feeling more confident about the mouth part.

"Well, that depends on how much you like the guy and how far you plan on going." I knew how much I liked Justin, but I didn't think we'd be rounding many of the bases in front of all the people at the aquarium. "Why don't you put them on his back or on his hips or on his face," she said. "That part should come pretty naturally. I'm trying to think back to the first time I kissed someone." Think back? This was so humiliating. Someone the same age as me was having a senior moment because it had been so long since she had her first kiss.

"That's OK," I said. "I think I got it." I wanted to stop talking about it so I could lie on my bed and envision the actual act of kissing Justin. Wouldn't it be the most amazing thing if it actually happened?

AFTER DOCTOR MEETING

Shit. I just found out the worst thing. Dr. Asshole told me that I'm going home on Friday. How can I go home already? I just got here! What have they even done to fix my problems? Nothing! I don't want to see my parents this soon, not after they locked me up here. And what about Sandy? What is she going to do here without me to be her friend? What about Matt O.? He's become a really good friend, too. And Justin. What about Justin? My first chance that a gorgeous guy could possibly like me, and I'll never know because I'm leaving. Then I'll go to my home and he'll stay here and fall in love with the next girl who moves onto the floor.

I'm crying. I've been crying since my doctor told me. I haven't cried in a couple of weeks, and now I'm doing it again. This place is horrible. How can they lock me up and force me to become close with all of these cool people and then rip me away from them again? Dr. Asshole said there was nothing I could do to stay. He said my insurance only covered twenty-one days, but that I seemed fine anyway so it shouldn't make a difference. The insurance. So my parents didn't put out for the super-sized policy.

Only three weeks. Is that enough time to fix a person?

TWO MINUTES LATER

Maybe I am fixed. There's no way I would have ever thrown a doll and screamed at the top of my lungs before I came here. And I never would have befriended most of the people here in my normal life, because I would've been too shy or insecure. I never would have crushed on a beautiful boy and believed in the possibility of him liking me. And I certainly never would have considered trying to kiss him, which I still am considering because Dr. Asshole informed me that I am still at Level III. "Why not," he said. "Go on the field trip." So I am going to kiss Justin. At this point, what do I have to lose?

SCHOOL

It seems that once the staff knows you're leaving, they don't care what you do. Justin and I sat next to each other at school today, looking over his architectural drawings, and no one told me to move. I wanted to be happy just sitting there next to Justin, but I was so sad that I'd only have a short time left to be with him.

I told him I was going to leave soon.

"What? But you just got here." He tapped his pen against the table with his right hand.

"How long have you been here?" I asked.

"It'll be a month tomorrow." I watched his right hand, the stitched one, clumsily write his name.

"Is that why you're here?" I nodded my head towards his hand.

"Yeah, it is." There was a pause, but I was afraid if I spoke I'd stop him from telling me anything. He went on, "I used to play the bass. Did I tell you that? In a punk band." No wonder I was so attracted to him! "We were called The Dipsticks. Not great, I know, but we were starting to get some gigs. We practiced in my garage, next to my dad's enormous collection of power tools. My dad hated the music, and he hated us using his space. 'You're pissing your life away!' he'd yell at me. He wanted me to be a carpenter, like him, but I want to design houses, not build them. Maybe even the band could've made it big." Justin flicked his pen against the table, hard. I had never seen him angry, and a part of me was afraid he'd lose it.

"One day when we were supposed to have practice I went into the garage. Instead of my friends, my dad was in there. 'I sent them home,' he said. 'I'm going to teach you something useful to do in the garage.' He started giving me a lecture on the table saw, but I didn't want to listen. I didn't give a shit about being a carpenter. All I could think about was how The Dipsticks needed to practice for an upcoming show. I ran bass lines in my head as he talked. Then he told me to come over, for me to try. I didn't want him to lecture me about the importance of listening, too, so I pretended I heard him." Justin dropped his pen, and it rolled off the edge of the table. "I ruined everything." He pushed the heels of his hands to his eyes. "The saw was harder to use than I thought. I slipped, and it cut right through."

Justin held his right hand out in front of us. "My dad picked up the pieces of my fingers and drove me to the hospital. They sewed them back on, but they still don't work right." He bent down to pick up his pen, his fingers clamped awkwardly around it. "They aren't strong enough to hold a pen, and they weren't strong enough to pull a trigger."

My eyes bugged. "A trigger for what?"

"I couldn't handle it, not being able to play my bass or write or draw. My dad keeps a gun in his nightstand. My fingers were so fucked up, I couldn't even kill myself when I wanted to. So I gave up on everything. No more band. No more bass. I can't even listen to it."

"You tried to kill yourself?" No matter how many times I thought about it, I never actually tried. "And *that's* why you only listen to The Doors."

No.

Bass.

"Pretty bad, huh?"

"You're not bad, Justin. None of us are." No one here, even total shitheads like Phil and Tanya, are truly bad. We just aren't who everyone else wants us to be.

I looked around to see if any teachers were near us, then I ran my fingers over his scars.

He carefully gripped his pen and wrote *Anna* next to his name. We stared at the letters together until school was over.

PLAY THERAPY

Flaky Play Therapy again. I couldn't even get excited to be spending the afternoon with Justin. I mean, of course I was happy he was there, but all I could think about were two things: 1) I will be leaving in less than two days and I'll probably never see him again and 2) I was going to be kissing this godly creature tomorrow and I was petrified.

We played a couple of games today in Play Therapy. Lady Big 'Do led the group in a rousing game of "How are we feeling today?" All of us sat in a circle (shocking!) on the floor and pretended to roll an imaginary ball to each other. Whoever pretend-caught the ball had to answer the question "How are we feeling today?" Sandy started us off. I thought she would say something about "losing her baby," but instead she said, "I'm sad because Anna is leaving on Friday."

"Damn," Victor shook his head.

Big 'Do said, "Let's take our turns, everyone. Wait until someone rolls the ball to you."

Sandy rolled the ball to Victor. "Damn," he repeated. "I'm sad 'cause I just found out Anna is leaving." Victor rolled the ball to Colby.

"I feel pretty good. I haven't heard any voices in over a week." Well, it's not like Colby and I ever really hung out. I couldn't expect everyone to be sad about *me*, could I? Colby rolled the ball to Justin.

"I'm truly bummed that Anna's leaving." He sad-smiled at me, and then rolled the ball my way.

"And what about you, Anna?" Big 'Do asked. "Are you at least happy to be going home?"

"No," I answered. "I'm not." Tears uncontrollably rolled down my cheeks.

"Well." Big 'Do bounced up, trying to sound cheery. "Let's liven things up a bit. Stand up in your circle. It's time for freeze dance!"

I hadn't freeze-danced since I was little. Big 'Do had a portable mini CD player/radio with one speaker. She turned the radio on to a hip-hop station and reminded us of the rules of the game. "When you hear the music: dance. When it stops: stop dancing. Try not to pay attention to anyone around you. Don't be embarrassed. Free your mind!" As the music started, we were all pretty dance-shy. Then on the radio a funky voice came on and announced an "Old Skool Jam," and that excellent song "Bust a Move" came on. All of a sudden everyone got into it. I'm not the best dancer, but it was pretty fun. Justin looked hot as he busted out some robotic moves. Colby did some weird gyrating dance, and Sandy performed one of her cheerleading routines. The music stopped abruptly, but it had been playing for so long that none of us even remembered it was a game of freeze dance. Eventually everyone started slowing down and looking around, and the momentum stopped. Just as each one of us became completely frozen, the music started again and we jammed the afternoon away.

Finally we were doing something that we all did in the real world! I love to dance, even though I'm usually doing it alone in my bedroom. But even at the lame school mixers that I occasionally drag myself to, I'm not opposed to getting my groove on. I wish we could do this every day at Lake Shit, but I can't imagine the adults would agree that instead of actual therapy, all we really needed was a dance party. My props to Big 'Do.

AFTER DINNER

Everyone at dinner was really surprised to hear I was leaving. Matt O. seemed particularly upset. "Everyone always leaves," he said. "It sucks."

"I wish I could stay," I told him.

"You do? Why?"

"Because what do I have to go home to? My parents don't even want to deal with me, which is why I'm here. There are only, like, three people at school that I even like. And I'll miss you guys," I said and peeked over at Justin's facial response. He just looked at his food.

"But you can do anything when you leave," Matt O. said dreamily. "You can eat anything you want and stay up late and watch movies and TV shows that you actually want to see. You can call and talk to and touch people whenever you want. You can breathe real air."

Did I sound like an idiot because I wanted to stay locked up in a mental hospital? Matt O.'s reasons for leaving made sense, but they didn't replace my reasons for staying. "At least you'll get to breathe real air tomorrow when we go on our field trip," I said to him. "And they told me we can order anything we want to eat at the aquarium cafeteria."

"I can't wait," Justin said. Wow. He can't wait. That's like beyond being just excited. Does he know what's going to happen? Does he know about my kissing plan? How could he know? He was probably just talking about the fresh air and the food. Or maybe not?

"I can't wait either," I said. I stopped eating my burger at that point because I got nervous anticipating the kiss. But it wasn't panic attack, Irritable Bowel Syndrome nervous. It was real teenager, butterflies-in-the-stomach nervous. My first kiss! With a hot guy! Oh God, please let it work out!

BEDTIME

Sandy demonstrated, and I practiced, kissing some more before bed. I wanted to make sure I was ready and that everything seemed natural. I tried to cover every possibility of a screwup.

"What if I have bad breath?" I asked.

"Chew on some gum," she said.

"What if I can't find his tongue?"

"Back off on your tongue until you feel his."

"What if he throws up in my mouth?"

"Um, that would just be gross."

OK. I was covered. Tomorrow will be the greatest single day

so far in my insignificant life. Hopefully there will be no vomit involved.

Thursday, Day 21
BFT (BEFORE FIELD TRIP)

This is it—the big day. I made sure to wear my somewhat-fitted black T-shirt that says, "The Circus Is in Town," to give the slight illusion of sexiness, although it's not nearly as clingy as it used to be. I wonder if my boobs are getting smaller. I borrowed a little hair gel from Sandy so the wave in my hair wouldn't frizz for the final touch.

Breakfast went by really slowly. Matt O. was pumped. "I'm so stoked, man; I never get out of here. Plus, I love sharks."

"Do they have sharks at the Shedd Aquarium?" Justin asked.

"Yeah. They have this whole reef thing where you get to walk underneath a glass fish tank while sharks swim over your head. It's way scary," I told him. My parents took me there right after the shark exhibit opened, and my sister and I ran under the sharks as fast as we could, screaming. I kept telling Mara that there were drops of water on the floor, which meant the shark tank was probably leaking and any minute the glass would shatter and the sharks would burst out and eat us. Even though I made it up to scare her, I kind of scared myself into believing it.

After we finished eating, everyone was supposed to wait in their rooms until we were called to the check-in desk. When they called, "School!" I didn't have to go. Ten minutes later

I heard Big 'Do's calming voice, "Anna . . . Justin . . . Matt O., please meet me in the front area." I was thrilled to hear her voice and not Eugene's. I quickly re-brushed my teeth for the fifty-seventh time, checked my nose in the mirror for boogs, and scrunched my hair for added curl. K-Day had finally arrived (that's Kiss Day, duh). A full report of today's events will follow as soon as I return.

AFT (AFTER FIELD TRIP)

Oh god. What an amazing, bizarre, unbelievable day. Here's what went down:

Justin, Matt O., and I met Big 'Do by the check-in desk. She carried a clipboard and hid several pens in her hair, which she randomly removed every time she needed to check something off.

"Ready to go?" she smiled. We all nodded, and she noted it with check marks. After she wedged the pen into her hair, we were off.

The elevator ride down to the first floor was quiet. Since there were only four of us, it would have looked weird if any of us stood too close to each other. No elevator action today, but I wasn't worried.

As we walked out through the front hallway of the building, I had flashbacks of the night my parents brought me in. Things looked different, since the daylight made everything brighter and cheerier. But I also felt I had a different perspective on the way things looked, too. At the beginning, I was scared and wussy.

Now I was the queen of our floor, a kick-ass Level III who also spent a little time in the Quiet Room for bad behavior. I had a feeling of superiority walking through the foyer, almost thuglike, as if the sight of me struck fear in the hearts of the crazies and old people who littered the hallway. I wish real life had Level IIIs.

Outside, the light was overpowering. Real, direct sunlight cannot be replaced with fluorescent bulbs and a screen-covered window. For the first time I saw how pale everyone looked, almost blue. Justin and Matt O. had poofy bags under their eyes, and Matt O.'s hair was a flat, grayish-black color I never noticed inside. I worried that they were picking out my faults, too, but we began walking, and soon the sun started soaking into my skin. My whole body felt five degrees warmer, but in a good, nonsweaty way. Big 'Do walked us to a busy intersection, stuck out her hair, er, arm, and caught a cab. She sat in the front seat, which allowed me automatic leg access to Justin. I sat in the small middle seat. You know when you sit in the middle seat next to someone you're really close to, so you lean your leg against them without even thinking about it? Or how when you're next to someone you don't know very well, you keep your leg tense the whole time so it doesn't touch theirs? Well, on the Matt O. side I could sense the tension from him, and every time we turned a corner and our legs accidentally touched, he jerked away. On the Justin side, at first our legs weren't touching. There was kind of enough room to not have to touch, especially with Matt O. backed into a corner. But when the first abrupt cab turn happened, and Justin was forcefully slid in my direction, our legs touched and didn't stop touching for the rest of the cab ride.

Big 'Do sat in the front, chatting away with the cab driver, who kept nodding and looking at the fare meter. When we got to the museum, 'Do said to us, "Be sure to get out on the curb side," and she handed the money to the driver.

The Shedd Aquarium is a beautiful, old building in itself, but the view of Chicago and the shores of Lake Michigan was like a postcard. I looked for Lake Shit amongst the skyscrapers, but I had only seen the outside of it twice. The city was endless in every direction, but all I could think of was how I had been in the exact same place for almost three weeks. In the back of my mind, I worried that a stomachache was coming on, but I took a deep breath and let all of the excitement and anticipation push that away.

"Everyone is so quiet." Big 'Do looked at us. Robotically we hadn't said a word since we left our rooms. I had assumed that the rules were the same on our field trip as they were at the hospital, and talking, unless told to, was forbidden. "It's OK if you talk to each other. This is your reward for doing such a good job in your treatment," Big 'Do said. Treatment. What an icky, sickly word. But seeing the pale faces of my friends, I guess it was fitting.

Justin, Matt O., and I looked at each other. With all of that freedom to talk, we didn't know what to say.

"Um, hi?" I said to both of them.

"Hi, yourself," Justin said, and if I wasn't such a petrified, inexperienced wuss, I would've kissed him right there.

"I hear that we're allowed to buy and eat any foods we want on this field trip. Is that correct?" Matt O. asked Big 'Do.

"As long as you don't go overboard, I don't see why not."

"Then I propose we begin with ice cream novelties."

"Matt, it's ten thirty in the morning," Justin told him.

"And your point is?"

"Lead the way," I said. Who could argue with ice cream novelties?

Outside of the aquarium was a man on an ice cream bicycle cart. He reminded me of Chilly Willy, the man who rode his bicycle cart every summer day through my subdivision at home. "What can I get ya?"

Matt O. ordered a SpongeBob Popsicle, while I opted for a Chipwich. Justin chose a Screwball, and Big 'Do surprised us all by ordering a Choco Taco. Before I ate, I wondered if Justin thought I was a cow for eating ice cream at 10:30 in the morning. But he was eating it, too, and it looked way too good to pass up.

While I enjoyed the ice cream immensely, I worried how it would make my breath smell. I hoped at some point there would be the option of gum. Like an answer to my prayers, Big 'Do pulled a pack of sugarless mint gum out of her purse. "Gum, anyone? It helps protect your teeth if you don't have a toothbrush handy." I gladly accepted, even though Big 'Do was freaking me out with her impression of a Stepford Wife.

We finally walked into the aquarium, and it was just as I remembered it: the same damp and fishy smell, the cavernous echo of hundreds of voices as kids and parents yelled, and the giant gift shop where I was always compelled to purchase fish-themed jewelry. I couldn't believe I was there with my two mental hospital inmates and a therapeutic chaperone.

The rest of the morning was spent looking at fish displays from all over the world. For some reason I didn't feel as bad for the fish as I normally feel for animals in zoos. I mean, the fish were trapped in these little water areas when they should have been living in the vast foreverness of oceans, lakes, and rivers, but they were so expressionless it was hard to feel pity. Did they know they were trapped? Were they sad? Content? Bored? They did kind of look bored. Actually, they looked pretty bor*ing.* After an hour of watching what looked like the same fish in different display cases, Matt O. declared, "I'm hungry. Can we get lunch?" Was he hungry from looking at fish? I began to wonder what kind of food they served in the cafeteria and just how fresh it was. Thankfully, the caf was filled with the usual crap that all museums serve: pizza, salads, and pre-made sandwiches with too much mayo. My decision was bittersweet: I would finally have a chance to eat pizza, my absolute, 100% favorite food in the entire world, but ordering reminded me that since I would be leaving on Friday morning, I would miss the Level III pizza party.

"The pizza party pizza supposedly tastes like turds anyway," Justin assured me as he ordered a cheese burrito and French fries. Matt O. ordered a chef salad, tuna sandwich, and an enchilada. "Well, they said anything. . . ."

I thought our lunch conversation would have been about the cab ride or the fish we just saw, but we really just talked about mental hospital things.

"How's Sandy doing?"

"Has Colby heard any voices lately?"

"Do you think Troy and Callie have done it?" This last question from Matt O. sparked a concerned look from Big 'Do, and I heard a thud as Matt O. jerked back from Justin's under-table kick.

"Who'd like to see the shark reef?" Big 'Do asked us. We all agreed that that would be very cool. I asked her for another piece of gum. "Last one," she said. That meant if I wanted to keep my minty fresh breath until the moment of kissage, I would have to limit my number of chews. I am one of those people who can't stand chewing hard gum, and I normally spit it out the second I sense stiffness. This time, I would be more careful.

To get to the shark reef, we had to take an elevator down to the bottom floor. The elevator was crowded with civilians, or at least non-crazies, which allowed for me to squish up against Justin. I looked at him and smiled a silly smile, and he gave me one of his closed-mouth hottie smiles. When would I find a moment alone with him?

The shark reef exhibit was dark and cool. It really did have a sense of doom, as if you never knew when a shark would turn on the humans, break the glass, and attack. The exhibit itself was made up of a winding pathway, where you could observe smaller sharks, read facts, and touch fake pieces of sharks' bodies. We began walking as a group of four, commenting to everyone as we observed new things. As we entered the shark tunnel, I looked up to watch the sharks swarm directly above my head. I swore I could hear their strong noses bumping up against the glass. When I looked back down, Matt O. and Big 'Do had walked farther into the exhibit. I was left behind with Justin. Was Matt O. doing that on purpose? Was he leading her away so that I could make my big move? He didn't even know I *had* a big move. Even if it was just a coincidence, I wouldn't let the chance escape. Matt O. and Big 'Do were far enough ahead that they had turned a corner. Justin and I were completely out of their sight.

I noticed then that the gum in my mouth had turned solid and rubbery, and I had to get rid of it. I found a garbage can nearby. Unfortunately, the gum was so dry that when I took it out of my mouth it immediately stuck to my fingers. As I tried desperately to get it off without it sticking to any more fingers, Justin approached me. This was not how it was supposed to go, I thought. He's going to see what a dork I am, and Big 'Do's going to notice we're gone while I waste my time trying to get this stupid gum off my fingers!

Justin watched me, smiling. I finally managed to stick the gum from my hand onto the side of the garbage can. "There!" I said, and I was ready to try the kiss. My heart was pounding in my stomach, in a good, crushy way. I tried to calm myself down by breathing deeply, and I was about to look up at Justin when the most perfect thing happened. Justin placed two of his fingers under my chin and tilted my head up towards his. Without even giving me a second to figure out what to do, Justin leaned forward and kissed me. And, naturally, I kissed him back. His kisses were warm and soft and slow. When he used his tongue (a few kisses after the initial kiss) it felt a little like his tongue was stroking mine. I didn't even have to think about where to put my hands; one automatically moved to his hip, which felt solid and manly, and the other to his cheek. I leaned back against the rocky exhibit wall, and we kissed and kissed and kissed. I opened one eye, and I swear that the sharks were doing a choreographed celebratory dance over our heads.

The moment broke when I heard Matt O. say my name loudly. "ANNA," and Justin pulled away from me. Instantly he pretended to read a display card, while Matt O. and Big 'Do rounded the corner back towards us. I heard Matt say to Big 'Do, "Yeah, ANNA has been a great friend at the hospital. We're gonna miss her."

Matt O. had given us a warning. That meant that he knew what we were doing. That meant that Justin had planned the whole thing and told Matt O. about it. Justin told Matt O. that he was going to kiss me. Kiss. I just kissed the most perfect, beautiful, sensitive guy in the world, and he made the first move. The most perfect, beautiful, sensitive guy in the world kissed *me.*

I floated through the rest of the field trip. When Matt O.

suggested we get another snack before leaving, I said I wasn't hungry. Justin said he wasn't either, but that didn't deter Matt O. from getting a blue snow cone and a pack of Sour Patch Kids.

The cab ride home was as quiet as the cab ride to the aquarium; even Big 'Do was too tired to talk. Justin took my left hand in his right hand, and I rubbed my thumb over his scars. My hand was a little bit clammy, but his was, too. Neither of us seemed to mind.

We got back to our rooms while everyone else was down at dinner. Matt O. asked to go down to the cafeteria to eat, but Justin and I said we were fine just hanging out in our rooms until Free Time.

When Sandy came back from dinner, I told her about the day's events, and the two of us jumped up and down and silently screamed. "I knew it!" she said. "I had a dream about this last night! Except you weren't at the aquarium, you were at the planetarium. And instead of Justin, you were kissing Phil, but still!" We laughed, and I lay down on top of my covers. Tonight would be my last Free Time with Justin. I closed my eyes and relived the kiss over and over, opening my eyes every once in a while to make sure Sandy wasn't watching me. Who knows if I accidentally kissed the air while I thought about it?

BEDTIME

Free Time tonight was stressful and disappointing. I wanted to touch Justin so badly now that I truly knew he wanted to touch me, too, but I couldn't. I didn't want to get him in trouble. I will be going home tomorrow, and good or bad behavior, my Level will disappear. Justin's won't.

Matt O., Sandy, Justin, and I played a quiet last game of Hearts. Justin and I touched legs, but it wasn't as sexy as it was comforting. It took a lot of effort for me not to bust out crying as we played.

Before Free Time ended, Justin slid his notebook across the table. "Write your phone number down, so I can call you if I ever get out of here." I scribbled my phone number and tried to think of something sincere, like what I'd write on the back of a school photo, to sum up all of my feelings for him over the past three weeks. Bettina interrupted with, "Free Time's over," and all I could get down was my name with a small, messy heart next to it.

We trudged down the hallway to our rooms, and I envisioned a passionate kiss with Justin where he throws me against a wall and grinds up against me. That didn't happen, of course, and a squeeze on my pinky from Justin brought me back to reality.

Sandy and I stood at our meshy window for the last night. I looked out at our getaway cars for the last time. Amazingly, there were people standing around them. It was too dark to see who they were, but I'd like to think that I saw an outline of a space helmet and the glint of a shiny silver space suit.

Whoever was there used a third car to jump the pastel cars, and soon the getaway cars were gone. So much for our escape.

But I don't have to escape. They are making me leave. I am going home tomorrow.

Friday, the Last Day

I woke up before the night crew came to get Sandy and me for our showers. I walked to the window and pushed my hand on the screen. I waited long enough that a grille formed on my fingertips. New fingerprints for the new person I have become.

I had hoped that the getaway cars had been moved back to their spots in the weird hotel parking lot across the street, but the spots were empty. A van pulled under the hotel awning, dropped off a few boxes, and then pulled away.

One of my ideas for my last day was to take a really long shower, and if anyone told me to get out I'd tell them to fuck off. But I had gotten so used to showering in such a short amount of time that my rebellious plan wasn't really necessary.

As I walked back to my room, I asked Sparkle what time I would be leaving. She told me that my parents were coming to pick me up after morning Community. That meant I'd have breakfast and Community to see Justin and my friends before I left. Maybe I would never see them again.

AFTER BREAKFAST

Breakfast was a bummer. I tried to liven it up with promises of mailing everyone cakes with nail files in them, but no one really laughed. Victor asked Justin, Matt O., and me about our field trip. I felt my face get hot, and I looked at Justin, who was as red as I felt. Matt O. told everyone, "A good time was had by all. Very educational." I smiled and shoved a spoonful of Cap'n Crunch in my mouth.

"So you'll really write? Who knows how much longer I'll be in here." Justin's dark eyes looked hopeful. I told him I would write, of course, although I wasn't sure he'd get my letters. "Why not?" he asked.

" 'Cause I haven't gotten any mail since I've been here. It's like everyone back home forgot about me."

"Nah, that's not why," Matt O. explained. "Sometimes people are put on a plan where they're not supposed to have any contact with the real world back home. Maybe you got mail, and they just didn't give it to you."

I was a little mad, but mostly confused. I did a lot of writing while I was here, but I never managed to send any of it away. Pencil or not, writing everything down was pretty important. Proof I was here, that I did all of this weird shit. And anyway, why would Tracy or anybody else back home want to hear about what I did in a mental hospital every day for three weeks? In turn, what good would it have done me to hear about all of the lame-o stuff that happened back home? It's not like anything there ever changes. The question is: How am I going to fit in when I get back? It's like I was transported to a parallel dimension while everyone else stayed in the normal world. I am a different person now. Will I ever belong anywhere as much as I did here?

THE END OF MY LAST DAY

Sandy helped me pack up my meager mental hospital belongings. We divided up the portraits; I took the ones of her, she kept the ones of me. I told her I was leaving her my juice lid collection and any newspaper pictures she wanted. I also gave her the colored pencils Mrs. Downy sent me. We thought it best to hug in our room, since we weren't sure how soon after Community I would be leaving. I had to take deep stomach breaths to try to stop myself from crying, but I couldn't help it. I never had a roommate before. I never had a fake pregnant friend before. Maybe I would never see her again. Sandy didn't really cry, but maybe all of the acting she did over Morgan had drained her of any real emotion. She did make a frown face, though, to coincide with my bawling.

"Community!" a voice yelled down the hall. I quickly went into the bathroom and threw cool water on my eyes. I dried off and tried to make myself as presentable as I could. I wanted to be remembered looking juicy, not like a blubbering, drowned rat.

Down the hall in the Day Room, I sat down on a green chair. Instead of gingerly placing myself on it to avoid the embarrassing sound, I plunked myself down and enjoyed my last stint in a fart chair. Pathetically, it actually made me chuckle. Justin sat in the chair directly opposite me in our circle.

Eugene began, "Since this will be Anna's last Community, we will start by saying our goodbyes. When I call on you, stand up and say something nice." For those who didn't know me well, it was very much like a standard yearbook autograph: "Have a good year. It was nice knowing you," and similar, impersonal statements.

Victor was somewhat more sentimental. "Anna, I'm gonna miss having you here. You were real sweet and funny, and you always laughed at my jokes." I smiled at Victor and realized he was probably the first black friend I'd ever really had, considering there were all of two black people in my high school.

Matt O. was next. "Anna, you are one of the best people that have ever been here. And I should know, since I'm probably going to be here for the rest of my life." He looked down. "Anyway, I'm going to miss you. Good luck in the real world."

"Sandy," Eugene called.

Sandy stood up. "I'm going to really miss having you as a roommate. You have been the best friend to me here, and I don't think I could have gotten through the last two weeks without you. I'm gonna miss sharing snacks and our getaway cars and our weird room games. I hope we can keep in touch." Sandy teared up, which made me tear up, and she quickly sat down. Her chair farted boisterously, and everyone laughed. That stopped me from crying for the moment.

It was Justin's turn. I don't know why Eugene saved him for last. Maybe he knew about us and was trying to build dramatic tension, or maybe he knew Justin always said nice things and wanted to save the best for last. Or maybe he was just going in order of the seats, and I was overthinking it.

Justin stood up and smiled at me. I couldn't see his eyes very well through the strands of his bangs, but I swore they were shinier than usual. "Anna," he squeaked, as if he were still going through puberty. He cleared his throat and tried again. "Anna, I don't really know how to say goodbye to you. You have become a really good friend, and I feel like I have more in common with you than anyone here. I hope when you go home you won't forget me. I hope if I ever get out of here we can go for coffee or something sometime. So, take care, and listen to The Doors for me when you get home, OK?" Everyone laughed, and he sat down.

The rest of Community was a blur of Restrictions, Appreciations, and Announcements. I didn't really pay attention. I thought about what Justin had said. How could I forget about him? At the same time, would we ever really go out for coffee? Would he want to hang out with me when he has normal friends at home to hang out with? By that time, would I be back to my normal life? I didn't want to think about him going to the grocery store or to a movie theater or meeting my mom. Do we belong together in the real world? It could never feel as special and intense as it did here in a mental hospital. That's why I didn't want to leave. My future boyfriends (god willing) won't have to be secrets. I can see them and talk to them and touch them whenever I want. Justin is my forbidden, secret love, and he can only be that way at Lakeland. That all ends today.

At the end of Community, everyone stood up to leave. That

was the last moment I would ever have to see Justin as we were. My desperation and rebellion took over. As Justin walked past me, I grabbed his arm and pulled him towards me. His body bumped against mine, and I looked up at him. I put my hand behind his neck, stood on my toes, and pulled his lips to mine. We got in about three good open-mouthed kisses before Eugene grabbed Justin's arm away and said, "Hey! Hey! That's enough! That's a Restriction for you, Justin." Justin shrugged. As I walked down the hallway to get my stuff, I looked back at him. He lifted his right hand and gave a small wave. I turned away and saw my parents.

OUTSIDE

My mother embraced me and cried, and I gave her a limp hug back. "You look so thin, honey."

"So glad you noticed, Mom." Three weeks away, and my fat is the most important thing she can talk about?

My dad patted my shoulder and gave me a nervous smile. He took my bags and headed for the elevator. Before I stepped in, the desk staff said goodbye and handed me a big, puffy, brown envelope. I waited until I got in the car to see what it was.

"Where's Mara?" I asked. I longed to see my sister, the neutral party.

"School," my mom answered.

This wasn't an event big enough to take Mara out of school?

My parents listened to a Cubs game during the drive home. It seemed completely bizarre that after locking me away for three weeks my parents had nothing more to say to me than when I left. I expected nothing more from my dad, but Mom . . .

That's when I noticed her shoulders shaking and realized she was crying. And not just crying—she was sobbing. I didn't know what she was feeling—guilty? Happy I was coming home? Happy I lost weight? At least she felt something. Her bawling was strangely comforting. But that didn't mean I wanted to deal with it. No more than they wanted to deal with me anyway.

I opened the big, brown envelope. Inside were about twenty envelopes, filled with letters and cards from different friends and family members (of course about half were from Tracy). I opened the fatter ones first, as those were the letters from my friends telling me about things going on at school and how much they missed me. I skimmed them, though, because I wasn't really that interested. Then I began to open the cards. One by one, I read them. They all said the same thing on the front: Get Well Soon. People sent me get well soon cards while I was in a mental hospital. There were fluffy little bunnies, floaty rainbows, and even a religious card. I could understand that Hallmark probably doesn't make "Get Sane Soon" cards, but still. Was I not well before? Am I well now? Who decides?

HOME

I'm home. At least, I'm at the house I grew up in, the bedroom that was designated as mine. But it doesn't look like my room anymore. While I was gone, my parents changed everything. The posters are gone. The collages are gone. Even the clown border is gone. They replaced everything with placid, pink, anti-suicide paint. My mom explained, "We thought you might like a change."

"And you thought *destroying my bedroom* would make me feel better?" I looked around for my posters, and found them in a pile on the floor in the corner, the blue Fun-Tac sticking each poster to the other like a giant punk poster sandwich. "My posters! Some of them are really rare! I can't believe you let them stick together!"

I ran over and began carefully peeling the posters apart. "This one's ripped! It was my favorite."

I fumed on the floor, and I began to notice something new: I wasn't crying. I was angry. Crying used to be my first reaction to anything and everything that upset me, and here I was, super-pissed.

I stood up. "You can't just do things to me and think I'm going to be OK with it!" I yelled.

"We thought you might like it," my mother answered meekly.

"Then you don't know me at all!" I picked up my alarm clock from my nightstand and threw it straight down on the floor. The face cracked off, and a few plastic pieces rolled around.

My mom stared at me, shocked. *I* was shocked. I had never done anything like that in my life. I never would have thought to.

I looked down at the broken alarm clock. "Shit," I said. I knelt to pick up the pieces. Perhaps I went a little overboard in "expressing my feelings."

My mom relaxed, probably glad to see I hadn't turned into a complete psycho, and said, "I'm heading to the store. I can pick you up a new alarm clock. Do you need anything else?" She smiled at me. Amazing. I'd been home for ten minutes, and already she wanted to get away from me. Whatever. We both needed some time.

I thought about what else I *needed*, all of those things I wanted at Lake Shit but I couldn't have.

"Cap'n Crunch, please."

"Cap'n Crunch," she said, with the slightest hesitation. Her eyes got shiny, and I could tell she wanted to say something dramatic about how happy she was to have me home. It would have been a perfect moment for an Appreciation, if we had those in real life: *Mom, I appreciate that you care about me, even though you're not very good at showing it.*

As she left, the phone rang. My dad picked up downstairs and a second later called, "Anna—Tracy's on the phone."

"Can you tell her I'll call her back in a few minutes?" I yelled down. I couldn't wait to talk to her, to really tell her everything that happened, but I needed a few minutes in my room.

I walked over to my stereo and turned the dial to a classic rock station. Like magic, a Doors song filled the air. Closing my eyes, I imagined sitting in the Day Room with Justin and all of my new friends. Friends who I would probably never see again, but could never forget. I opened my eyes to pink walls. Gag. The first thing Tracy and I would do together is paint away the pink and put my posters back up. But for now, I lay down on top of my new bedspread, and looked forward to my life.

ACKNOWLEDGMENTS

Big, giant thanks go out to the following people:

Mom and Dad, who are NOT the parents in this book (per Mom's request).

My sister, Amy, the bestest sis on Earth.

The rest of my family, near and far, for being so supportive.

My cat, Tobin, who I am pretty sure can read this book.

My students: Eastman, Maisie, Julia, and Samantha, who read my book before it was anything and made me feel like a writer, and to all of my students, past, present, and future, who inspire me and make me laugh every day.

Beth, who read the book on command when I needed her to, and my friends Tracy, Susannah, and Cheryl, for reading and cheering me on.

Metra Rail and Warren-Newport Library, for giving me places to write.

My editor, Liz, for giving me this amazing opportunity and making the revision process fun, regardless of how many random, unbook-related e-mails I have sent her.

And Matt, who gets a dedication *and* an acknowledgment, 'cause he's my husband and best friend.

Thank you for reading this FEIWEL and FRIENDS book.

The FRIENDS who made *Get Well Soon* possible are:

Jean Feiwel, *Publisher*

Liz Szabla, *Editor-in-Chief*

Rich Deas, *Creative Director*

Elizabeth Fithian, *Marketing Director*

Elizabeth Usuriello, *Assistant to the Publisher*

Dave Barrett, *Managing Editor*

Nicole Liebowitz Moulaison, *Production Manager*

Find out more about our authors and artists and our future publishing at www.feiwelandfriends.com.

Our Books are Friends for Life